EMPIRE OF EVIL

By
ROBERT ARNETTE
(aka Rog Phillips)

I0616776

ARMCHAIR FICTION
PO Box 4369, Medford, Oregon   97501-0168

For more information about Armchair Books and products, visit our website at...

www.armchairfiction.com

Or email us at...

armchairfiction@yahoo.com

KIDNAPPED TO VENUS!

It was a truly horrible situation—marauding alien pirates from Venus were looting the heartlands of America and the rest of the world almost at will. Not only did they make off with a fortune in valuable booty, but their most prized pickings were untold numbers of unsuspecting Earth women. These were beautiful women, too—women who were lusted after by unsavory creatures from Earth's planetary neighbors.

So it was left to two of Earth's best Intelligence agents to solve the problem. Their mission was to find the secret location of a powerful force field that protected a vast Venusian city filled with space raiders. Space raiders who, if left unchecked, would continue to ravage and eventually destroy Earth.

FOR A COMPLETE SECOND NOVEL, TURN TO PAGE 89

CAST OF CHARACTERS

RON KRATNICK
He was way down on the list. Not the best agent to take on a tough job like this, but all the others ahead of him were dead!

GLORY EVANS
She was kidnapped—stark naked—by alien raiders. Would she be able to survive as a sex slave on another planet?

TANTON
He was the best agent Earth had for a daring plot that would save the planet—and he hadn't been heard from in months!

MARGOT
This beautiful princess led a life of vast wealth. All she had to do in return was give her body to a powerful alien brute!

TZA-NECROS
This four-armed monstrosity ruled an entire underworld on the planet Venus. He also had a one-hundred-year old mistress!

VALCAN
As head of the Venusian Secret Service it was possible for him to bend the rules, especially when it came to beautiful women.

CALIBAN
He was a powerful thug in an underworld filled with the scum of the Earth—and his best bargaining chip was a beautiful woman.

CHAPTER ONE

A BLUE Mercurian, arrogance in every line of his shell-covered body, was leading a white Earth girl up the street. The Earth girl was practically naked. She walked with head bent, shoulders drooping—a creature without hope. The rope around her slender waist, by which the Mercurian hauled her along, had raised a cruel, circular abrasion on her otherwise smooth brown skin.

The girl stumbled and the Mercurian jerked ruthlessly at the rope just as a pair of Darrien's black-tailed Venusian fighters paused in passing to grin and lay lascivious hands upon the girl's body.

The Mercurian snarled and yanked the girl away. "Mine!" he spat, and laid a hand on the zam-gun at his belt. He pushed the girl behind him and faced the two Venusians, ready to kill or be killed in defense of his rare prize.

Ordinarily there would have been quick death here—either one Mercurian spilling out his green blood on the walk, or two Venusians stiff in death, their black tails twitching and snapping. The Venusians, who considered themselves the aristocrats of Darrien's hideous army, had more than once taken loot from their fellow fighters from the other planets. And this young virgin was a prize indeed.

But the Venusians were sated at the moment. Their bellies were full of raw flesh and warming Bizant liquor. So they laughed and moved on, much to the Mercurian's surprise.

Seated at a cafe table nearby, Ron Kratnick was fighting with himself as he had never fought before, battling to hold his fury in check, striving to keep from leaping forward to tear the Mercurian's dome-shaped head from his shoulders.

EMPIRE OF

By Robert Arnette

All that stood between Earth and final destruction was a creature from Mercury which no one trusted

"Flog her!" Tsa-Necros screamed. "No woman can be unfaithful to me—and live!"

EVIL

Bright in Ron's senses was the vision of what was going to happen to this girl. Apparently fresh from Earth, probably from America, she had no doubt been taken in one of the rapier-like raids of Darrien's forces and, according to the code of Darrien, she was fair loot of the blue Mercurian soldier.

Ron Kratnick writhed inwardly as he thought of Darrien—that archfiend of the universe, thought of the man's devilish cleverness in discovering the one thing that would make his interplanetary army fight like tigers possessed—the promise of Earth women as their own property, to be used as they saw fit. The girl, beyond doubt, would be better off dead.

But Ron held himself in by conjuring up the words of Blake Wentworth, Chief of Universal Intelligence: "You'll see some terrible things on Venus, Kratnick. Things done to our women and to captive soldiers that will make your blood boil and well nigh unseat your reason. Your ability to control yourself will be the mark of your success or failure. When you see a girl raped or tortured, you've got to remember that you can do nothing for her—that your allegiance lies with the millions here on Earth—that your success will mean salvation for them. When you get to Venus, you've got to ignore everything except your prime objective."

Kratnick's mind then flashed back for several minutes to that pivotal conversation with Wentworth, and then to the series of events that led up to his present circumstance...

"And what is that objective?" Ron asked Wentworth. He'd been called, completely unbriefed, from an assignment in Africa, and had come to Chicago with no idea whatever as to what his orders would contain.

Blake Wentworth, a highly capable, but sorely harassed Intelligence Chief, smiled bitterly. "I'll come to that, but first, let me give you the background." Wentworth's smile twisted into deeper bitterness as he snatched a cigarette from the tray on his desk. "Most of it you know, of course, so we'll just call it blowing off steam on my part. A man's got to sound off once in a while, or the stuff piles up inside him and cracks him up."

"I understand, sir."

"To a certain extent, maybe, but you can't know how I feel. You can't possibly know because you haven't been in the saddle—taking the abuse for the mistakes made by others."

There was sympathy in Ron's smile, "I'm a good listener, sir."

"The trouble with this planet, Kratnick, is that they were too cocky. The chosen people and all that silly rot. It came on gradually of course. With the most advanced brains in the universe, we naturally were the superiors of the barbaric peoples we found on other planets. Our technical know-how was such that we had no trouble controlling them. And as time went on we considered ourselves the paternal lords of the universe. The High Council members got up off their fat lard buckets and spouted off about how the, blue Mercurians and the Venusians and the Martians loved us and looked to us for guidance."

This was evidently a subject close to Wentworth's heart because he mashed his cigarette into a tray and his eyes blazed. "*Loved* us! Any fool with half an eye could see they hated our guts, envied our advancements and drooled down their tusks at thoughts of getting us by the throats."

Ron said nothing. There didn't seem to be anything to say. Wentworth scowled at his subordinate much as though he considered it his blame and then went on.

"Then we came up with that foul scheme for getting rid of our own trash and scum. Send them to Venus! Take our mobsters and degenerates and murderers and foist them off on the Venusians, and if the Venusians didn't like it—the hell with them! I remember when a pompous ass of a hypocrite named Lanson made the suggestion to the High Council. I can remember his very words…"

Wentworth had unconsciously burlesqued the voice and attitude of a typical well-fed politician: "Fellow citizens, why should the sweet air of earth be polluted by the breath of such as these? Let's send them to consort with their own kind—the savages in the red jungles of Venus. Let that steaming red planet fulfill the destiny for which it was created—let it be our penal colony."

The Intelligence Chief stopped for lack of breath and Ron felt caned upon to say something. "That was quite a while ago. I was just a kid then."

"Yes and I was still a young man when that groundwork for today's hellishness was laid. But I was in the Service when Darrien reared his rotten head and had to be dealt with."

"That I remember clearly," Ron said. "It was a big issue in the press. After his two attempts to overthrow the government I remember there was a great public clamor for his execution."

"I was a part of that clamor," Wentworth replied grimly. "I went before a Council committee and testified that regardless of Darrien's general rottenness, he had one of the greatest brains of all time, that by sending him to the penal colony of Venusia, we were sewing the seeds of our own possible destruction."

"But they sent him there anyhow."

WENTWORTH'S mood had changed from one of fire to one of moody defeat. "That's right. My words meant nothing and the Council went along with the sob sisters and the so-called humanitarians. As a result, we lighted a time bomb that's going off now. Darrien went to work immediately. Just because certain men are criminals doesn't mean they have no brains. Darrien combed the cesspools of the universe and came up with brains by the bucketful. In ten years he built a war machine that has us with our backs to the wall. He built the most ferocious army ever conceived by the simple process of offering his soldiers our women as prizes."

It was Ron's turn to frown. "But, sir, we aren't exactly helpless. We have four space fleets, anyone of which is capable of blowing Venusia out into the void. I'm just an agent and I don't know what happens on the inside, but I know that's what the public is howling about. They want to know why we haven't done just that—blown Darrien's rat's-nest to Kingdom Come. Your talk of our having our backs to the wall surprises me, I didn't know it was that bad."

"And neither does the public," Wentworth said grimly. "They blame the Council for not stopping the Earth-raids of Darrien's space ships. That's impossible unless we destroy Venusia."

"Then why don't we?"

"Because we can't."

It was equivalent to saying a man couldn't slap a fly on his own wrist. Ron allowed his expression to mirror surprise but said nothing.

Wentworth lit another cigarette and blew a cloud of smoke through his nose. He then asked, "Did you ever hear of the Clanton Space Mine?"

Ron shook his head and Wentworth smiled without humor. "If you had," Wentworth said, "it would mean a leak in Intelligence. Very few people know about it. If the information got out, there'd be panic in the streets."

He punched a button on his desk. A door opened at the far end of the room and a young man entered. The young man had about him the impersonal air of the scientist. He crossed the room and stood by Wentworth's desk, staring at the Chief—through calm, impersonal eyes. Wentworth closed his own eyes, evidently from sheer weariness.

"This is Corbett," he said. "One of our brilliant young brains, Corbett, tell this man about the Clanton Space Mine."

While Wentworth appeared to sleep, the young scientist turned to Ron and spoke in a flat voice as though he were reading his words off a sheet of paper:

"The Clanton Space Mine can be compared, for the sake of understanding its function, to the explosive land mines used in ancient wars to blow up a road over which the enemy was passing. It is used for exactly the same purpose relative to a ship passing through a given area of space. It is an entirely invisible and unregisterable—"

Ron held up a hand. "What do you mean by unregisterable?"

"That its presence cannot be detected by any instruments—at least by any instruments we have been able to devise."

"I see."

"This mine consists of a ray and was discovered by Andrew Clanton—"

WENTWORTH was evidently not asleep because he waved an impatient hand without opening his eyes and said, "The hell with that. Everybody knows Clanton is a scaly-legged genius Darrien picked up in a Martian booze house. Tell him how they use the mine."

The youth went on: "To the best of our knowledge, the ray emanates from a central power plant located in the city of Venusia. It is projected so that it forms an umbrella over the city and about seven hundred square miles surrounding it. Functionally, this ray umbrella explodes any missile, lethal or otherwise, which comes down into its area of effectiveness. That area, so far as we can ascertain, has a depth of about a mile and lies about two hundred miles above the city and surrounding jungles."

"Remember that, Kratnick," Wentworth said, still without opening his eyes. "Seven good men died getting us that information."

There was a moment of silence, after which Wentworth said, "All right. Tell him the rest."

"We know also that there are entrances—tunnels so to speak, through this umbrella—uncontaminated passages in space through which Darrien's ships can enter and exit safely."

"But," Wentworth cut in, "we don't know where they are."

"Is that all, sir?" the young scientist asked. Wentworth nodded and then Corbett left the room.

"You know the score now, Kratnick," Wentworth said. "You know why Darrien's been holding us helpless. If we can't get through that umbrella with a bombardment squadron, these raids will continue until Earth is in panic and Darrien has recruited enough emboldened fighters from other planets to come down and annihilate us."

"I see why you call the situation serious," Ron said grimly. "What are my orders?"

"They're pretty much equivalent to suicide. I want you to go in and locate that projection plant and put it out of commission."

"Might I ask—why I was picked for the job?"

"On your record." Wentworth hesitated, then spoke with an added grimness in his voice. "You're entitled to the truth, Kratnick. I told you seven men had already died in the project. They were all good, but that number includes Tanton, the Mercurian, I banked heavily on him but he's been gone for over four months now, and we're giving him up for dead. Anything Tanton couldn't crack is—well, almost impossible."

Ron was genuinely shocked upon hearing this news. Tanton! The blue Mercurian had been practically a legend among the men of Intelligence. A master of over fifty languages, a graduate of Cambridge and the Harvard

University of Advanced Theoretics, he was an unsurpassed nuclear physicist, a recognized composer and—this above all—an incurable adventurer. Why, it was an honor, even to be considered for a project on which the great Tanton had failed!

"And there were six others beside Tanton?"

"Our best men right up the line. Three Earthmen, a Martian, and two Plutonians. It's practically a certainty they're all dead. Probably died in agony after being tortured. You may certainly refuse the assignment if you wish."

"How do I get through the umbrella?"

"As a member of a Venusian raiding party. At times we get information as to where a raiding party intends to strike. Not very often but when we do, we use that information pretty grimly—we allow the raid to be made and use it to plant an agent in Venusia."

Ron understood instantly and his stomach tightened in protest at the seeming callousness. Darrien's forces were allowed to make off with a number of Earthlings in order that Intelligence could make a stab at winning this grim struggle. The unfortunates who were captured became hapless pawns in a game that was for keeps—a game where the stakes ran into the millions of lives.

"I know what you're thinking," Wentworth said, "I know it seems treacherous and rotten, but in this business you've got to weigh all the evils and condone the lightest in order to smash the heaviest."

"I understand," Ron said.

"The Raiders come in lots of about five hundred—usually only one ship—and are a mixture from every planet. Fortunately for us, Darrien has recruited a battalion of Earth-men-renegade exiles from our slums and cesspools. We've managed to capture a few of these and when the raid is staged, you're to infiltrate into the marauders. If necessary in order to carry it off—snatch yourself a woman captive and take her back to Venusia."

"I'll be entirely upon my own of course."

"Entirely. One of our space fleets is patrolling continuously off Venusia. We'll give you their wave length and you're to notify them if you succeed in destroying the projector."

Wentworth got to his feet and held out his hand. "And I promise you," he said grimly, "if you can do it, there'll be a big hole in Venus immediately thereafter."

"I'll try my best, sir," Ron said, and shook Wentworth's hand. He left, terribly sorry for this man who had to sit at a desk with the weight of the whole terrible affair on his shoulders, this man who perhaps saw in his dreams the faces of Earthlings sacrificed in a plan he himself had devised.

"Good luck, Kratnick," Wentworth said.

"Thank you, sir," Ron replied. Crouched in some bushes two nights later on the outskirts of a small town in Iowa, Kratnick had listened to the chirping of crickets in a nearby swamp and searched the dark skies for signs of a spaceship. He was clad in the tight gray britches and red tunic of Darrien's Earthmen Brigade. He wore the leather harness that distinguished those renegades, and he carried a zam-gun on his hip. In a supply packet at his belt were papers— genuine enough—identifying him as Louis Diehl, a young St. Louis embezzler who had been exiled to Venusia, had returned as one of Darrien's raiders, and was now safely put away in the cell blocks in Chicago. Ron also wore, on his tunic, the tiny, almost imperceptible blue stitching that would identify him for what he was to any agent he chanced to meet.

But I won't meet any, he told himself. *They're all dead and I'm the eighth in line.*

The red tail of a spaceship appeared in the sky, Ron crouched in the bushes and thought of Tanton.

CHAPTER TWO

TANTON'S greatest asset was a sixth sense, which was uncanny in warning the blue Mercurian of danger. The moment he had set foot on Venusian soil, this sense rang a signal bell—told him point-blank that he was being watched.

Possessed of the azure, shell-skin of all Mercurians, he was incapable of facial expression, but his round eyes searched every face in the vicinity and finally settled upon two Venusian idlers in civilian garb who were lounging nearby in entirely too casual a manner. Had Tanton been capable of smiling, he would have done so now. What stupid ass had put these two dolts on his trail?

As he shuffled away from the Earth-raiding space ship after it had set down in its homeport with its warriors and their booty, his mind went swiftly to work.

Starting with the knowledge that he was being watched, he began milling over the facts in his mind. First, it was obvious that he'd been spotted for what he was—an Earth Intelligence Agent. Therefore, his presence on the spaceship was known even before he left Earth with the raiders.

Armed with this knowledge, he moved into line with the raiders who were waiting to be numbered off before having their loot returned to them, and was struck by the fact that the two Venusians made no move to collar him. This gave him something more to build upon.

Obviously they had been told to watch him rather than to make an arrest. With this thought in view, he moved casually out of the line and drifted toward the gate of the enclosure, certain that no one would detain him.

The two Secret Service men drifted also toward the gate

and followed Tanton up the street. Tanton, moving casually, and with no apparent destination, made it very easy for them. He avoided crowded streets and wandered up into the second tier of the city and stood for a time gazing up at the vast glass dome that covered Venusia. This dome, one of the greatest architectural feats in history, covered twenty-five square miles and shut out the vast heat of the flaming sun, thus turning Venusia into an air-conditioned city. Tanton gawked up at it like the most naive tourist, keeping careful sight on his spotters the while.

Absolutely certain of his facts now, he returned to the first tier, had a leisurely dinner, and then moved off toward a certain intersection at the west end of the city. He knew exactly where he was going, although he certainly did not appear to.

So, when he was quite ready, he shook off the two Secret Service men by the execution of one quick maneuver, redoubled his pace, and went straight to an ancient stone building where he found a door, a door cleverly camouflaged with dust, debris, and apparent disuse.

He knocked on the door, his knock a staccato of taps, obviously in code. Then he lounged against the wall and awaited results.

Ten years prior to this time, he had gone through exactly the same movements and now—as then—the results were identical. After five minutes, a small window opened in the door-panel and a red, hostile eye peered out.

"I'm Tanton," the agent said. "I want to see the princess."

These words he had also used ten years before and now the same, hideous misshapen creature drew back the panel and croaked that he should enter.

WITHIN, Tanton found a small room lit by a dusty levon tube that, barring deliberate or accidental damage, would burn forever. The incredibly filthy one-eyed creature who acted as doorkeeper apparently recognized Tanton—acted in fact, as though ten years was hardly longer than ten minutes. The thing held out a scaly hand and gave with what was intended to be a grin. "One creda," it mouthed. "One creda for food."

Tanton laid a silver coin—a three-creda piece—into the hand and was rewarded with a frenzied little dance as the creature showed its appreciation. As Tanton crossed the room and went down a flight of stairs into the murky levels below, the creature was still registering happiness.

Tanton moved swiftly, entirely sure of himself. He was in a tunnel now that stretched off into the distance, illuminated at irregular intervals by levon tubes, and with other tunnels branching off it every few hundred feet.

This was the famed Undercity of Venusia, a tunneled and catacombed area of unmapped crypts and death traps with a history so gory as to make even the Casbah of olden times pale into positive respectability.

Here, like slavering rats in the darkness, lived the vermin that had been rejected by the greater body of vermin exiled from Earth. In these passages dwelt the absolute dregs of the universe. Even members of Darrien's intrepid Secret Police had been known to resign rather than pursue a criminal into these deadly labyrinths.

A complete shadow-government was known to exist down here. The King of the Undercity was reputed to be a four-armed freak named Tza-Necros from the Planetoids, where evolution sometimes went wild and produced all manner of fantastic animal forms. This monster, possessed of a fine brain in his repulsive cask of a head, had created the shadow-empire himself and stood out successfully against even the ruthless Darrien who was said to have recoiled in horror at accounts of what went on in the Undercity. Twice Darrien had attempted to clean out the foul nest, too strong even for his stomach, and as a result, several thousand of his men now lay rotting in the dark tunnels below.

Tanton, however, seemed entirely at home. He moved with a sure step from one passage to another. He walked with zam-gun in hand and coldly alert when coming abreast of a cross-passage or to a place where the tunnel ceiling vaulted away and left room for balconies giving on the tunnel itself.

He was entirely conscious of the hungry eyes that followed his progress but he found that no creature barred his way.

The passages were taking him ever downward and it seemed, finally, that he must be at least a mile under the first tier of the city above him. Then he stopped abruptly, examined a wall on his right, and tapped it sharply with the butt of his zam-gun. He waited for ten minutes, after which time, the routine at the first entrance, high above, was repeated.

Again Tanton said, "I want to see the Princess."

There was no hesitancy on the part of this doorkeeper, a young Plutonian with a zam-gun of his own clutched in his fin-like hand.

The room inside was cleaner this time, and furnished with deeply upholstered chairs and a thick white yangskin rug.

THE AGENT stepped inside, showing neither hesitancy nor even a ghost of caution. "Tell the Princess that Tanton is here. Make it quick or I'll strip off your hide and push it down your throat."

This was evidently language the young guard understood, because, with a surly growl, he pocketed his gun and went out through another door.

A few moments later he returned, and Tanton was ushered through the inner door.

There was the sound of tinkling fountains, the music of rippling water, an artificial sky of lazy blue with white clouds floating by. A pathway of yellow brick led off through this amazing paradise, winding through rows of palm trees and banks of carefully tended flowers.

Tanton hesitated for a moment and then a voice called out to him: "Here, Tanton—over here."

The blue Mercurian moved in that direction and came to a fern-rimmed pool out of which there arose a golden flame of a girl, completely naked, to stand on tip-toe in the lush grass and shake water from her long blonde hair.

Tanton sat down on a marble, bench close by. As a sign of friendship, he removed his harness and dropped it in the grass.

"It's been a long time, Tanton," the girl said, "Throw me the towel there, and my robe."

Tanton picked up both articles and carried them to the girl. He stood by while she dried her brown body and slipped into a robe of fluffy gold-flecked material.

"You're in trouble of course," the girl said, laughing, "or you wouldn't have come."

"I'm in trouble—yes—but that's got nothing to do with it. Your callousness wounds me."

She laughed again as they made their way back to the bench. Tanton sat down and the girl dropped into the grass at his feet and sat looking up at him. "Tell me the news. What goes on back on Earth and around the Universe?"

"He still keeps you cut off from things then?"

For a moment her mask of gayety slipped and Tanton could see the bleak unhappiness underneath. He had met this girl, long years before, in a New York cafe. She'd been a dancer then and when this paradise in the heart of Venusia's Undercity had been offered her—with certain strings attached—she'd taken it in lieu of a more strenuous life on

Earth.

Margot had not changed one iota through the years. This, however, did not surprise Tanton. Rather, he'd have been surprised to find signs of age, what with Margot's access to the youth hormones developed in Kordo's Martian laboratories.

"Yes," the girl said, "I'm trapped here, but he's good to me. He's kept his end of the bargain and I've kept mine." She smiled and waved a hand in the direction of the pool and the glittering apartments beyond the garden. "What other girl has had what I've had? I live in the most beautiful place in the Universe. My every wish is granted. I have fifty people to fulfill my slightest whim, I'm the luckiest girl ever born."

"You're trying hard to convince yourself of that, aren't you?" Tanton said. Margot dropped her eyes and Tanton went on: "Can anything compensate for the ordeals you go through with that four-armed monstrosity from the Planetoids?"

MARGOT laid a hand on Tanton's armored knee. Her eyes were still downcast. "Tza-Necros is good to me," she said. But she could not hide the hopelessness in her voice. "If it wasn't for him I'd be an ancient hag by now. I was over a hundred years old when I stopped counting. He got the hormones for me that give me eternal youth. I have complete mastery here in my buried Eden. He gives me what other girls only dream of having and all he asks in return is my—love."

"He hasn't got your love and he knows it. All he has is your body."

Margot raised her head in a flare of defiance. "Well—isn't that little enough?"

Tanton put a hand under her chin and kept her from again lowering her head. He stared into her lovely face until she cast her eyes down. "Why don't you stop trying to kid an old friend," he said softly.

"It's *his* body, isn't it?" she whispered glancing down at her golden torso. "He's kept it young."

"Stop it."

The girl held her poise for a few more moments. Then it cracked and she flung herself down to bury her face in Tanton's harness and burst into a frenzy of weeping.

Tanton sat motionless watching her. Possibly a little pity was mirrored in his round eyes, but more probably not. Tanton came of a realistic race and was not given to emotion.

When her sobs had diminished, he reached down and lifted her to the bench and sat her down beside him, "That's better," he said, "You've been a lot of things in your lifetime, Margot, but never a hypocrite. Now stop the blubbering and tell me about it."

She looked at him—dry-eyed now—her face oddly expressionless. "Damn you to hellfire," she said, dully. "May God spit in your stupid eyes. I should have you killed and use your skull for a flowerpot. But—I can't."

"Of course you can't. One doesn't kill old friends. Besides, my skull would poison the flowers. Tell me—how long have you felt this way? How long have you been fed up?"

There was utter hopelessness in her voice, "I've always hated it, but for the last five years it's been—horrible. I can't seem to steel myself against it any more. Those—those four hairy arms—that slavering mouth!" She lowered her head into her hands for a moment, then raised her head and there was a hard smile on her face.

"Sorry, I'm trapped here and there's no escape. But tell me about yourself. What news of the outside world?"

But Tanton's mind was not on world events. He had no inclination whatever to turn himself into a walking newspaper. Instead, the wily Mercurian was evolving plans of his own. Already, his brain was busy building a ladder of intrigue and double dealing up which he could climb to his objective—the destruction of Darrien's ray projector. He was no lily-white crusader, this Mercurian. He had learned his business in a hard school and it wasn't by chance that he was one of the cleverest agents in Earth's employ. His one saving grace was utter loyalty to whatever cause he served. His reason for serving a cause was entirely a selfish one—for example he was an Earth Intelligence agent because it was the most lucrative proposition he could find for his peculiar talents.

Nor was there any high-mindedness in the loyalty he gave after casting his lot with a particular group. It was simply a matter of common sense and good business. An untrustworthy agent would soon find himself out of a job, whereas a loyal one increased his reputation and, it followed, his monetary value.

SO NOW, with a structure of intrigue forming in his mind, he laid his first groundwork, "Have you ever taken a lover?" he asked. "Some man a trifle more palatable than your four-armed friend?"

Margot shook her head. "No. I've lived up to my part of the bargain. It's the last shred of decency left to me."

"I'm sorry you feel that way," Tanton said. "Any man in Venusia would sell his soul for two hours with you."

"That may be true," Margot said without ostentation, "but it makes no difference."

"If you'd be a little more reasonable, I think I could get you out of here. Back to earth where you'd be safe from Tza-Necros."

The shot, fired at the girl when her guard was down, brought quick blood. She grasped Tanton's hand. "You—

you could get me *out?*" In her eyes was wild entreaty. Then she caught herself and her shoulders drooped. "You talk foolishness, my friend."

"You should know me better than that. I don't babble for the sake of hearing my own voice. I said I could get you out and I can—safely."

"But what would my taking a lover have to do with it?"

Tanton did not answer for a moment. His mind raced through the names of Darrien's bullyboys until he came to Lars Valcan, head of the grim and bloody Secret Service. This feared branch of officialdom was vested with the duty of counteracting espionage and ferreting out dissenters in every form; also with the protection of government installations. Beyond doubt, Valcan would know the location of the ray projector.

"Would you be willing to spend a half hour with Lars Valcan?" Tanton: asked, "That is if I could in turn promise you safe passage back to Earth?"

"How would that help?"

"It's merely a matter of enlisting powerful friends," Tanton lied glibly. "Valcan wouldn't help us for any amount of money. But for the privilege of holding you in his arms. To be able to talk of it later—"

Margot, even in her degradation, had the grace to flush.

"In less than three months you could be walking the streets of New York City," Tanton said. "Riding across the good green land—breathing Earth air and bathing in the blessed sunlight."

Even then, Tanton knew he'd won. Even before Margot said, "I'll try it." Then, even more bitterly, "I guess I'm desperate enough to try anything."

Swiftly, Tanton followed up his advantage. "I'll be back in three hours at the most," he said. "Send orders to all entrances that I'm to be admitted no matter who is with me.

And you be waiting in the garden."

While talking, he had been snapping his harness on. Now he turned away and left as he had come, quitting the hidden paradise for the foul passages beyond. A short time later he was across the city, standing in front of a tall marble building that housed the offices of the Secret Police. He was entirely alone, his spotters not having picked him up after his exit from the Undercity.

HE STRODE boldly up the well-worn steps and into the lobby where a young Venusian with a built-in scowl and a zam-gun on either hip barred his way.

"I want to see Lars Valcan," he said. "Take me to him."

"You must be as stupid as you look," the Venusian snarled. "No one sees Lars Valcan—except maybe over the lip of a roasting pit."

"I'll see him. Tell him that Tanton, Intelligence agent from Earth wants an interview. And jump to it or you'll fry on a griddle before sundown."

The guard's mouth dropped open. Here was something utterly inconceivable. It couldn't be a joke because jokes weren't perpetrated within the walls of the Secret Police Building. Here all was grimness and stark reality. The guard walked slowly away, backwards, his eyes still on Tanton. The guard waved a hand and immediately four uniformed soldiers moved in from various locations about the lobby and formed a square around Tanton. The agent ignored them.

The guard backed up to a counter behind which two other officials were seated. He spoke to them in a low, voice over his shoulder. They came close to the counter, leaned over, and the three held a hurried conference, after which one of the officials snapped a switch and spoke into a mouthpiece.

After a few moments he got up and came around into the lobby toward Tanton. "This way," he said sharply.

With the four-man guard still in entourage, Tanton was escorted to a small room and placed before a visi-plate. There was a whining sound and the plate lit up to reveal a heavy-set, handsome Earthman seated at a desk. The man, frowning, remained silent.

"Greetings, Valcan," Tanton said easily, "When your two spotters got careless and lost me, I felt slighted. I'm certainly more important than that. I came to make inquiries and, incidentally, to do you a service."

The paths of these two had crossed before and Lars Valcan had no reason to love Tanton. But Tanton knew his man. He knew that Valcan, sure of his own position, would grant him an interview out of curiosity if nothing more. An interview was all Tanton asked.

"Send him up," Valcan growled and the plate went dead.

Tanton entered Valcan's office, threw his harness on the floor and took a chair beside the Secret Service Chief's desk. He was as much at ease as he would have been in the office of his own chief on Earth.

"Even though I'm going to have you tortured to death," Valcan said, "I've still got to admire your nerve—walking in here like this."

"I said I was here to do you a service."

Valcan smiled coldly, "How stupid do you think we are, Tanton? Let me tell you a little about yourself. You infiltrated into a party of our raiders near a small town in Maryland. You used the papers of a soldier, an Earthman, named Brad Wilcox who was captured on an earlier raid—"

"I threw the papers away before I boarded the spaceship," Tanton cut in. "I knew a man of your caliber wouldn't be fooled so easily."

"Don't interrupt me. Two men were put on you the moment you stepped on Venusian soil."

"And they lost me two hours later."

"Do you know why you weren't picked up? Do you know why all the Earth Intelligence agents who came before you weren't picked up until we were quite ready?"

"Of course. Darrien wants Earth to keep on sending agents until they run onto something. The S. S. lets them wander about as they please. It's Darrien's method of stalling for time. And do you know where I went after I shook off your spotters?"

"No," Valcan growled.

"I went down into the Undercity to report to my boss—to deliver him some documents from New York."

VALCAN showed genuine surprise.

"Your boss! Are you trying to make me believe you're working for Tza-Necros?"

"Of course I am, and I don't care whether you believe it or not—you will later. I got stranded in New York on an assignment when Earth suspended all flights to Venus. I had to get back, so what better way was there than to sign up with Earth Intelligence in order to get a ride?"

Valcan was no fool but his brain was not in the same league with that of Tanton. He smiled coldly and asked the question Tanton was waiting for, "Why did you have to join Intelligence to board one of our ships? You've slipped up, my friend."

"Your raids weren't exactly broadcast beforehand," Tanton answered, suavely. "Earth Intelligence was getting information on a few of your landings and I had to join up in order to locate one of your ships. Any fool should be able to figure that out."

If Tanton had been capable of smiling, he'd have done so now at Valcan's dark discomfiture. However, he allowed the Secret Service Chief no time for a reply.

"But that's not important. The important thing is that I've

got a proposition for you for Tza-Necros. The old boy's scared stiff."

Valcan was entirely disarmed by surprise and interest. "Tza-Necros? Scared of what?"

Calmly, Tanton threw his bombshell. "That new death ray Clanton invented. The one Darrien's going to use to clean out every living thing in the Undercity. Tza-Necros bought some information about it from a professional informer and he's in a panic. I understand Clanton can turn it into the underground tunnels and annihilate all life in twenty-four hours. That's true isn't it?"

Valcan was thinking fast, but still the clever Mercurian agent was able to follow the process of his adversary's thinking almost as easily as though Valcan had put it into words.

Up to this point, Valcan had been wondering whether or not Tanton had been lying about not being an Earth Intelligence agent. Now, so long as he had Tanton in his power, the point no longer mattered, but now it was overshadowed by the new information.

Granting that Tanton was working for Tza-Necros, it was both logical and possible that some sharp-witted informer had sold the Undercity dictator some silly rumors about the Clanton Space Mine. The secret was closely guarded and not one man in ten thousand knew the location, there in Venusia, of the ray projector. But rumors got about and it was entirely possible the thing had been rumored as a device to clean out the Undercity.

On the strength of this, and by some somewhat faulty reasoning, Valcan decided Tanton was also in the dark as to the true nature of the device.

"You mentioned a proposition," Valcan said coldly.

Tanton chuckled inwardly. "He'll give you a million credas in gold for the location of the ray projector."

"In other words, he takes me for a traitor."

Tanton sighed. "I didn't think you'd do it for mere gold," he said, "and neither did Tza-Necros. So he'll throw in Margot. That will give you an idea of how scared the old boy is."

"Then Margot really exists?" The golden girl, who lived in an Eden under Venusia, was in the realm of legend. Tales of her beauty and her ability to please her four-armed lord were legend, but no one was sure she was other than the dream of some hopped-up storyteller.

"Of course she exists, I've seen her myself. If you agree, I'm to take you down into the Undercity and show you the place Tza-Necros built for her. You can visit her down there or bring her out, whichever you choose."

Sore temptation beset Valcan just as Tanton knew it would. Valcan's reasoning ran thus. What did it matter if Tza-Necros knew the location of the ray projector? Once, he, Valcan, got the money and the fabulous Margot, he could see that Tza-Necros was acquainted with the true facts—that the projector in reality guarded Venusia from Earth's spaceships, and thus also guarded Tza-Necros' Undercity.

But Valcan brought himself up sharply. It was absurd, entirely absurd. But then again—Margot. The golden legend of the Undercity. Valcan yearned for the prestige that would go with acquiring her for himself—from parading her in the smart eating and drinking places of Venusia. But—

Abruptly, Valcan pressed a button on his desk. Three heavily armed guards entered the room. Valcan pointed at the blue Mercurian agent.

"Put him in a cell," he snapped. "I'll make out the execution orders for early tomorrow morning."

Tanton was lead away, and at that moment his faith in his own powers fell to zero.

CHAPTER THREE

AS RON KRATNICK watched the dark skies over Iowa, the fiery tail he'd observed, brightened, and a silver ship rocketed down out of space.

Immediately lights began flashing on in the village nearby, but not before the great shining globe from Venus, coming in a long, graceful sweep, had set down on the meadowland of Iowa.

Ramps shot out of the globe, doors opened automatically, and Darrien's hordes spewed forth. They were as motley a collection of demons as Ron had ever seen gathered in one place. First came a contingent of Darrien's pride—the evil, black-tailed Venusian fighting men, each carrying a zam-gun and armed also with the death-sting, swift and terrible, embedded at the end of those whipping, black posterior formations. Then came the blue Mercurian devils, the eyes in their shell-covered faces alight at the prospect of Earth women's bodies. Then came the ferocious Martian hillmen, thirsting for pillage and loot.

Like an ocean wave they frothed across the level ground full of the weird, eerie cries of other planets. The wave engulfed Ron and he rose up and went with it, became a part of it, and he told himself: Now I'm a renegade. I want a share of the loot Darrien promised me, my share of white Earth flesh. Think the part and the better I'll act it.

The invaders were smashing into houses now. There were terrified Earth screams added to the din, as the scene took on the horrible proportions of something straight out of hell. Appalled at the sight, Ron found himself frozen while the action milled about him. From the house in front of which he stood, three persons came running, a very old man, a middle-aged woman and a girl of perhaps eighteen, fleeing from a Martian hillman.

The Martian passed the elder two in one long stride and caught the terrorized girl by the arm. In desperation, the elder woman struck out at him only to go down, her skull crushed by the butt of the Martian's zam-gun. The old man stumbled and went headlong to receive a kick from the Martian, which doubled him up in agony.

Ron's stomach was revolting at the scene around him, women and girls dragged, partially clad or entirely naked, from houses, dragged by arms, legs, or hair, some thrown over the shoulders of the raiders to scream and twist and writhe helplessly.

I can't stand much of this, Ron told himself through gritted teeth. But I've *got* to stand it! Hold myself in!

Then, at the sight of two Venusians on down the street fighting over a cowering blonde girl, Ron realized there was something he could do—a small thing but it would keep him from going mad and blowing the whole deadly important assignment.

He leaped at a Martian hillman who now had a shrieking girl in his arms and knocked him spinning with one blow of his right fist. The surprised Martian went down, only to come up with a roar of rage, mouthing again and again the word that could be heard from all directions: "Mine—mine—mine!"

THE GIRL had fallen, too, and Ron caught her by the wrist as the Martian charged in, clawing for his zam-gun. Ron flung the girl behind him where she crouched, sobbing, with her face in her hands. He took the Martian's head-on charge on his lowered right shoulder. He heaved, fiercely happy at the feeling of impact, and hurled the hillman backward.

"Mine! Mine!" Ron shouted into the hillman's tusked mouth and jammed his zam-gun into the creature's gut. He snapped the switch and a great hole appeared in the hillman—a round, bloodless hole from which the Martian's bowels, heart and lungs had vanished into a sharp crackle of atomized dust. The Martian's lips came back off slavering teeth. He was dead but the horrible jaws still worked as he melted to the ground.

Ron whirled and slugged out at a blue Mercurian who was reaching for his nightgown-clad prize. The Mercurian snarled in protest, nursing the split shell on his right cheek. But he was not inclined to argue further and went hulking off in search of other loot.

Ron lifted the girl over his shoulder. As he carried her along he could feel her breasts and the agonized pounding of her heart against his neck. "Mine! Mine," he shouted in triumph as he passed other raiders intent upon their work. And it seemed to him that his smile must have resembled a leering, grinning skull.

The raid was in its final stages now. A horn had been sounded from the space ship and the raiders were streaming back toward the meadow. Some with live loot—others who had to be content with inanimate plunder—and some with empty hands.

But back they went because life, after all, was the dearest thing, and to be left behind meant certain death.

Ron lagged behind the streaming mob, snarling at the envious, empty-handed raiders. He allowed them to pass him by as he swung in a circle toward the comparative gloom of the bushes. With only a few raiders left to board the waiting ship, Ron set the girl on her feet, held her erect when she would have slipped down in heap.

"Run," he gritted in her ear. "Off that way into the

darkness! For God's sake—*run!*"

The stricken girl did not understand at first. Then she took a couple of faltering steps, tangled one foot in her torn nightgown, and went down, moaning.

Glancing desperately around, Ron yanked her to her feet. "Don't you understand me? Run!" With a sweep of his hand he tore away the entangling nightgown, leaving her stark naked. He jammed the garment into her hands and whispered. "Put it on later, but get away from here!" He gave her sharp slap on her bare bottom and had the satisfaction of seeing her come to life and turn into a blurred white streak to disappear into the gloom.

Whirling around, Ron dived for the space ship where only one ramp was still down. He scrambled up the ramp and got inside just as the door swung to and thudded into the heavy rubber jambs, leaving a smooth, unmarred surface on the outer shell of the ship.

Two Venusians pushed him aside and locked the inner door. Ron turned away quickly, hiding his face as much as possible, but it was evident the Venusians were paying him no attention. He hurried up the inner ramp, faced now with the first important hurdle of the assignment. He was impersonating a genuine Earth renegade. His papers were in order, but that renegade had not been aboard this ship at the start of its journey. For all Intelligence knew, its previous seven agents may have been spotted for what they were immediately upon boarding the raider's space ships. The trip to Venus was something more than a suburban jaunt and while there was probably no check made until the ship reached its port, a masquerader could be turned up by the men themselves. Associations were made on a trip of this sort. Men made friends with other men and were known. An unknown man would be a subject for investigation.

RON HAD a plan to at least partially overcome this danger. From foreknowledge, he knew the customs followed on such occasions as this. He knew the men were not allowed access to their booty during the flight back to Venus, at least not to the live booty!

The captive women were segregated in a separate compartment to be turned over to the soldiers upon arrival. This forestalled possible fights and death-struggles over the prizes en-route. It also allowed the officers much pleasure at their leisure. Things happened to the more desirable captives on the trip back—things Ron didn't dare think about.

And too, the soldiers themselves were segregated in small groups for the better handling thereof. Although it was not mandatory, the men congregated with their own kind. Martians usually traveled with Martians. The Venusians hung together and the Earth renegades, the most clannish of all, usually congregated by themselves. So Ron had decided to avoid the Earthmen who would no doubt turn him up as an interloper, and select other companions for his trip to Venusia.

He picked the most vicious of them all—the black-tailed Venusian warriors themselves. He followed a group of these into a compartment, tossed his harness on a bunk and prepared to snarl down any other claimant.

There were roughly twenty-five Venusians in the group, he estimated. Also he saw one Martian and a single Plutonian. The Martian, his tusks still bloody from the raid, took the bunk next to Ron and sat down to wind a piece of dirty cloth around a small ankle wound.

Ron stretched out in his bunk, closed his eyes and took a slow, deep breath. He had completed the first leg of his assignment. The ship was already in motion and soon there would be food for the victorious warriors. Then the Venusians would pile into their bunks and put themselves into a dream-state, a drug-induced stupor, for which purpose each Venusian carried a small bag of dried leaves from the Jadic bush—that evil, red vegetation which could be found only in the stifling Venusian jungles.

I wonder if I'll ever get there? Ron thought. I wonder how soon some alert officer will spot me?

I wonder how long I'll live?

When he finally went to sleep it was with the feeling that he would be yanked at any minute from his bunk and made to face a blinding light, while voices barked questions into his ears and heavy fists maimed him for not answering.

But he slept on and awakened to find food on the table. The Martian and the Plutonian were seated at the table. They'd just finished eating and were conversing in some outer planet language unfamiliar to Ron.

At the other end of the table a single Venusian was gnawing on a leg of beef, cracking the bone with his strong teeth to get at the marrow inside. As Ron watched, the Venusian growled to himself and returned to his bunk.

Ron got up and went to the table. The two from alien planets stopped talking and eyed him with hostility. He ignored them, filled a plate and satisfied his appetite.

JUST AS he was finishing his meal, the door opened and a Venusian entered. The man wore the distinctive harness of a high-ranking officer. He walked straight to the table and stood looking down at Ron. He remained silent as Ron tensed his muscles for what appeared to be a payoff. So this was what had happened to the other Intelligence men. Spotted even before they left Earth, they had each been jetted away to quick death in high space.

But the Venusian officer remained silent and made no motion toward Ron. He stood for a full minute staring down at Ron. Then he grinned—a knowing, wolfish grin—and went out as he had come.

Reaction set in and Ron felt suddenly weak. The Martian and the Plutonian, who had sat silent, their eyes on the tableau, now returned to their conversation. Ron got up from the table and went back to his bunk.

The episode left him bewildered. What lay behind it? He could have sworn the Venusian officer knew him for what he was. Yet the man had gone calmly about his business. Was it a cat and mouse game? Knowing they had Ron helpless, were they toying with him? Ron was inclined to doubt this. It wasn't the way Venusians did business. One thing was certain to Ron, however. He would never reach Venusia alive.

At least a dozen times during the trip, Ron was clinically— but silently inspected by men from the officers' quarters. Each time he prepared for the end and was set to do battle. But each time nothing transpired in the way of action. It was a bewildering thing and wore his nerves to raw edges. By the time the ship was ready to set down in its home berth he was as tense as a steel wire.

But again, nothing happened. He quitted the ship and mixed with the boisterous raiders in the bullpen prior to numbering off. No one, apparently, was paying him any attention whatever.

Now was the time, he decided. Certainly he wasn't going to stand around waiting for death. He moved casually toward a ramp, expecting, any moment, to be apprehended or shot down in his tracks.

No one barred his way. He achieved the enclosure beyond the ramp and mixed in with the Venusian citizens who were there to welcome the raiders home and feast their eyes on the white captives who would soon be led from the ship.

Ron moved through the crowd and toward the exit. He

found no one there to bar his way, and drifted out into the street. Now he increased his pace and quick elation surged through him. Apparently it had all been his imagination!

Then he discovered the two Venusians on his trail and realized the reverse was true. He had been spotted. He was definitely known as an Intelligence agent.

But what was the game? This question entered his mind after he had spent an hour moving around the city and knew, beyond doubt, that the men were following him. Did they expect him to lead them to someone? If so, to whom?

He debated the wisdom of attempting to elude them at this point or to wait for a more favorable opportunity. If he tried to get away from them and failed, they might arrest him then and there.

Mulling this question over in his mind, he found himself passing a sidewalk cafe on the first tier of a busy street. He dropped into a chair and saw his two spotters immediately stop and lean casually against a wall some fifty yards away.

When the waiter came, Ron ordered a bottle of Bizant liquor and drank a full glass without stopping. He had not slept well on the trip in from Earth, nor had he had much of an appetite. The liquor tightened his already raw nerves.

His whole being writhed for action. He was tired of the cat and mouse game. As a result of the liquor, he had a mighty urge to end this thing for good and all.

In short, he stopped thinking like an Intelligence agent, and when the blue Mercurian came along, dragging the white Earth girl by a rope, Ron had to fight with himself as he'd never fought before. His liquor-heated rage flared brightly and he gripped the table edge with both hands until his knuckles were white.

He sat with his teeth locked tight together as he watched the two Venusian soldiers paw the girl with obscene gestures. He waited for the explosion that didn't come.

Then, as the trouble passed over, and the blue Mercurian jerked cruelly at the rope, Ron lost his battle. He was out of his chair like a projectile. The hell with the assignment! The hell with everything. He had to twist off the arrogant head of that blue Mercurian or go completely berserk.

He heard a voice—his own—yelling, "You turtle-faced son-of-a-bitch! Leggo that rope!" as he dived straight at the blue man.

CHAPTER FOUR

TANTON, lying in comfort on the stone floor of his cell, was inclined to be philosophical about the whole thing. He had no fear of death, nor did he have any regrets. During all the years he'd played at his dangerous game, he'd known that someday this would happen. His wily intrigues, practiced to gain his own ends on practically every inhabitable planet, had always been successful. But he'd known that someday one would miss, and that he would be finished.

He was aware of his mistake in this case. He'd misjudged the Secret Service chief. The structure of his intrigue had been basically sound except for one flaw. He'd banked too strongly on Valcan's lust for the beautiful Margot—upon his greed for the prestige of acquiring her.

This he could only shrug off as a mistake and forget about it. It did irk him somewhat that he'd be marked in Earth Intelligence offices as having failed on an assignment. But that too was of no great importance. He wouldn't be around long to suffer the humiliation.

With this thought in mind, he went to sleep.

The following morning he was awake to hear footsteps in the hall. The roasting pit no doubt was now at the required high temperature. The footsteps stopped and the door opened.

But it was only a guard bearing a tray of food and a flacon of water. The guard set the food down and retired. Evidently, Tanton decided, they were going to feed him before roasting him. For this he was grateful and set to work upon the tray with gusto.

After eating, he went back to sleep. When he awoke, the

small window—high in his cell—was black. Night had come. The day of his execution had passed and he was still alive.

This surprised him. But as day after day passed in monotonous regularity and he saw no one but the silent guard with tray and flacon, his wonder increased with the time.

What had gone wrong? Then, suddenly, he knew and his faith in his own abilities shot sky-high. He hadn't failed. Not by any means, and he could sense the struggle going on in Valcan's mind—analyze it as accurately as though Valcan had come down to tell him about it.

The Secret Service chief was fighting between greed and fear. In the beginning, fear had been the stronger. Because of this he'd thrown Tanton into a cell, but the greed stayed his fingers, day after day, from signing the death warrant.

Tanton took a new lease on life and began wondering how long Valcan would hold out. The weeks became months and the months became four, with Tanton waxing fat and lazy in his cell.

It must be quite a battle, he told himself. I wonder how long he can hold out? The next morning there were footsteps in the hall as usual, but more brisk now, with a sound of more positive authority.

It was Valcan.

HE ENTERED the cell and stood down at Tanton who was stretched full length upon the floor. "It's been a long time," Tanton said.

"I couldn't make up my mind, I'm still not convinced that—"

"But you're ready to go ahead with it?"

Valcan glanced uneasily at the door, then continued speaking in a lower voice. "It's not as easy as you think. Especially now that you've been committed to jail. The best I can do is to see that you escape. I'll give your guard an order to show you an escape-route—a passage to the second tier of the street behind the building. Then, after you've escaped, I'll come down and kill him—for negligence of duty."

"A clever procedure," Tanton said, and was entirely sincere about it. He'd been guilty of equally treacherous deeds more than once in his career.

"But once you're beyond the walls, you'll have to fend for yourself. I'll have to put every man on the alert. And if you're captured you won't live long enough to make any accusations against me."

"Don't worry," Tanton said, cheerfully. "I'm not in the habit of getting caught."

"Then where can I meet you after you're clear?"

"What time is it?"

"A little after the thirteenth hour."

"Meet me, at the eighteenth hour on the first tier of Darrien Promenade and a small street called Antor. And come alone. Otherwise we will not be admitted to the Undercity."

Valcan was silent for a moment before he said, "I believe you said I could bring Margot out of the Undercity with me. Otherwise—"

"That will be your privilege. And you can also bring the million credas out."

"That is of no consequence, I already have well over ten million credas."

Tanton got to his feet. "Why don't you give me the location of the ray projector now?" he suggested. "It might save time, and will put Tza-Necros into a good mood to receive you."

"Do you think I'm a fool?"

"I was hoping you were, but I guess I'm wrong," Tanton said. "When will the guard come?"

"Within an hour," Valcan said. "And remember, you'll have not more than five minutes before the alarm will be sounded. Goodbye now—I hope we meet again."

"At the Promenade and Antor Street. The eighteenth hour."

Fifteen minutes later, Tanton was standing alone in the small alley behind the prison. Another five minutes and Valcan had personally slain Tanton's guard and had sounded the alarm for the agent's recapture.

Tanton moved swiftly in the few minutes of grace, but not swiftly enough. Before he could shoulder his way into a trans-city jet car, a master-switch was thrown at Secret Service Headquarters and every pilot obeyed the red signal to stop his car. A cordon was thrown around a mile-square area with the prison as its center. With a smoothness indicating long practice, the Service went into action, checking people out of the area, one by one, through turnstiles and ordering them not to return until the Service quitted the restricted area.

Tanton was neatly trapped.

And he knew what his fate would be if he were captured—quick death. Beyond doubt the Service men had been ordered to shoot him down instantly upon identification.

PAUSING on a side street to take his bearings, Tanton wracked his brain for a way out. But, while infinitely clever, he was not given to working miracles. His lightning brain reviewed the situation and gave a negative report. There was no way out. All the civilians in the area would be checked at the exits. Then the square mile would be combed by men walking elbow to elbow. No escape.

Tanton stepped back into a doorway as footsteps sounded on the deserted street. A moment later a lumbering giant of a man, a Martian, came around the corner and moved in

Tanton's direction. Pushing his head into view, Tanton saw, first the Martian, and then the practically naked Earth girl he was dragging along by means of a rope around the latter's slim waist.

Tanton catalogued the girl instantly. Obviously an American, she was no doubt from some town recently raided by the Venusians. The droop of her smooth shoulders and the fear and utter hopelessness in her eyes, marked her for what she was. Loot. A girl taken on a raid by the Martian, and now his property to do with as he saw fit.

Another point impressed Tanton. This Martian was evidently looking for a place of seclusion—some deserted nook or alleyway, where he could examine his prize in privacy.

Then a plan for salvation—his own salvation—was born in Tanton's mind. Had he been able to smile, he would have done so as he stepped from the doorway and moved toward the Martian and the captive girl.

The Martian, immediately suspicious, yanked the girl roughly forward and pushed her behind him as he scowled at Tanton. The latter walked up, a picture of innocent interest, and craned his neck to peer around the Martian. He noted, in doing so, the red welt of the rope completely encircling the waist of the lush Earth girl.

"A rare prize," Tanton said, "Is she for sale? I'll pay two hundred credas gold. A hundred and fifty platinum."

"Mine," the Martian snarled, "I took her in a raid."

"Of course she's yours, but I want to buy her. I'll pay."

The Martian considered for a moment. "I'll sell, but not now. Two days from now I'll return to this spot with her at the same time. Then I'll sell."

Tanton considered in turn, but the Martian had no idea what was in the Mercurian's mind. He had no credas on his person and no intention of buying the girl. Also he had no weapon. Hence the seeming thought on the Martian's proposition which was in reality, a ruse to get a trifle closer to the man—close enough to jerk the zam-gun from his harness.

Finally, Tanton shook his head. "No. I want her now— not after you've spoiled her. I'm not interested in second-hand goods. "I'll pay three hundred—gold."

The Martian did what Tanton had hoped he would do— turned his head to look appraisingly at the girl and consider whether he could find more pleasure with the money in some Venusian booze and flesh house, than with this slim brown Earth virgin.

He turned his head just enough for Tanton's arm to streak out and come back gripping the raider's zam-gun. The Martian whirled in alarm but his brain probably hadn't even time to form the fear-pattern because—in an instant—his head was gone, charred into a thimbleful of black crust by the ray from the zam-gun.

AS THE big body melted to the pavement, Tanton snatched the rope from the lifeless hand and said to the cowering girl; "You're mine now. See that you come along peacefully and keep your mouth shut. Otherwise I'll sell you in the first flesh house I come to."

The girl whimpered and lowered her head in complete defeat.

A few minutes later, Tanton, now apparently half-drunk, weaved his way toward one of the turnstiles set up by the Secret Service. He was shouting a ribald Mercurian drinking song and seemed surprised and bewildered upon finding a barricade.

"What's this?" he demanded of a young Service Lieutenant. "Who stands in the way of a soldier of Darrien? One side or I'll fry you."

The lieutenant's eyes were on the Earth girl as Tanton had

anticipated. To the young Venusian, Tanton was obviously a triumphant and most fortunate raider who was parading his booty for all to see. Pulling his hot eyes away from the girl, and scarcely looking at Tanton, the lieutenant glanced at the record sheet in his hand and waved Tanton through. As the girl followed, her arms folded to cover a portion of her nudity; she felt the hand of the lieutenant brush casually over her body. She shivered and responded to the jerk of the rope in Tanton's hand, "Come on, girl," Tanton said, "No one bars the way of an Earth raider."

Tanton gave the girl no rest as he hurried across the city. He was past the main danger now, but the whole Service had been alerted and he would possibly be challenged at any moment, though—thanks to his masquerade—it was doubtful.

He kept to the direct thoroughfare on the first tier, considering audacity to be a good thing and had no trouble until he was within a quarter-mile of his goal—the nearest entrance to the Undercity of which he had knowledge.

Thus, with safety almost in his grasp, he was intercepted by two swaggering Venusian fighters. Their lustful eyes brightened at sight of the girl and, as Tanton hauled her past them, their hands were upon her.

Here was possible trouble and it had to be met head-on. Tanton snarled as he yanked the girl toward him. "Mine", he spat, and gripped the butt of his zam-gun.

But the reaction of the Venusians was not as Tanton expected. They were in an amiable mood—rare for Venusians—and they laughed good-naturedly as they moved on. Tanton breathed a sigh of relief. A brawl at this point would have brought inquiries—inquiries fatal to Tanton.

Then, just as he was resuming his course, trouble sprang at him from another quarter. This in the form of an apparently demented Earthman—a handsome young man in the harness of Darrien's raiders, who dived straight at Tanton's throat from a cafe table nearby.

Tanton, unable to draw his gun, whirled to meet the charge and went down under the fury of the mad assault. He heard a thundering voice in his ear:

"You turtle-faced son-of-a-bitch! Leggo that rope."

Tanton's head cracked hard against the pavement but that bothered him not at all. His skull could not have been split with a hand axe, so thick and hard was its shell covering.

But he had a vulnerable point at his neck and the Earthman evidently knew this because he had Tanton's head gripped in both hands and was twisting it. Too much of this and the head would snap off at the base of the neck. Then the crazy Earthman could lift it away like a disconnected doorknob.

TANTON strained—heaved upward—and his eyes came into line with the Earthman's chest. There, almost invisible, was the faint blue stitching which marked him for what he was—an Earth Intelligence Agent.

It flashed swiftly through Tanton's mind that this man was a disgrace to his planet. He'd lost his head while on an assignment.

But that did not change the fact that Tanton was also close to losing his own head. He jerked the Earthman close to him and gritted. "Stop it you fool! Look at my tunic! I'm an agent myself. My name is Tanton!"

His words pierced the Earthman's brain and quieted the maniacal fury of his attack. His expression changed to one of bewilderment as he loosed his hold on Tanton's tortured head.

"We've got to get away from here quick," Tanton hissed. "The Service men will haul us to jail and we'll be lost. A crowd is gathering already."

Ron Kratnick saw that this was true. Passers-by had stopped to watch the fight and the walk was becoming crowded.

"I'll throw you off," Tanton whispered. "Then I'll get up and run with the girl. You follow us until you see me turn into an alley but don't catch up with us till then."

With this, the blue Mercurian executed a mighty heave, sending Ron Kratnick rolling into the gutter. Immediately, Ron doubled up as though in agony, as though a hidden blow had paralyzed him.

The Mercurian was on his feet instantly to gallop off down the street, dragging the whimpering girl behind him.

After a reasonable time, Ron got to his feet and ran after the fleeing Mercurian.

Ahead with the girl, Tanton found he could not travel very fast. The girl was bare-footed and was not used to running full-tilt through city streets. Then Tanton glanced back and found that the Earthman had developed a limp which retarded his progress. Thus the distance between them remained pretty much unchanged.

The second time he glanced back, Tanton saw something else. Two Venusians, obviously spotters who had been put on the Earthman's trail, had recovered from their surprise at the swift turn of events and were now in pursuit. Fortunately Venusians were slow of foot, but even so, the distance between them and the Earthman was fast diminishing. Tanton was happy to see that the Venusians had not drawn their weapons. Evidently they felt well able to catch the Earthman alive.

Tanton pulled cruelly on the rope, forcing the Earth girl to increased speed and it was with a feeling of relief that he came to the alley toward which he'd been running. He pulled the girl into the narrow passageway, then pushed his head around the edge of the building and looked back down the street.

The Earthman's limp had magically vanished and he was kiting up the street at a speed that caused the Venusians to claw for their zam-guns.

Then the Earthman was braking his speed to turn and slip into the alleyway past Tanton.

"What now?" Ron asked, gasping for breath.

"The spotters," Tanton said, his zam-gun already in his hand. "You take the short one. I'll cut the tall one in two."

AS THEY approached and hurled themselves into the alley's mouth, the two Venusians died instantly as rays from two zam-guns fried various parts of their anatomies into fragments of hard black crust.

As the men fell, Tanton stepped forward and sprayed the bodies with the zam-gun until there was nothing left of either one except a few fragments of crust.

Watching this brutal annihilation, the Earth girl sobbed and swayed against the wall, close to the end of her strength.

"I'm not doing this because I enjoy it," Tanton growled, "but we can't leave any remains to be discovered later. This is too close to an Undercity entrance. By the way," he said to Ron, as his zam-gun crackled out the consuming heat ray, "since when has Intelligence been hiring fools like you?"

Ron Kratnick flushed in the semidarkness of the alley. But he hurled back no defense at the insult because he had no defense. He'd acted the fool all right—the callow schoolboy—and the incident could easily end his career as an agent. "I—I don't know why I did it…" he said, "I knew those spotters were on me and I decided things were hopeless with all the other agents dead. I had to make one gesture of defiance before they killed me. This is my first assignment away from Earth and—"

"—and if you keep on the way you're going, it will be your

last," Tanton cut in. "What's your name?"

"Ronald Kratnick. I have an S-rating. Nine successful assignments."

"You must have been a devil for luck," Tanton observed sourly as he cleaned up the last of the unseared flesh on the ground. "And thank heaven I rate you so I won't have to beat a cocky young superior down to his natural size."

Ron felt heat rising within him at the Mercurian's tone and words. But he dampened it swiftly with the knowledge that he deserved censure. And too, this was the great Tanton. One took criticism from Earth's top agent and didn't resent it—at least not outwardly.

"I'll take your orders of course," Ron said, stiffly.

His work completed, Tanton turned and pointed to the girl. "You'd better carry her," he said. "She's about finished. You've got to get down into the Undercity before she can stop and rest. Better cut that rope off her."

"The Undercity?" Ron asked in surprise. He'd heard of rumors of that horrible place—tales of its cruelties and obscenities, but he'd never been really sure of its actual existence. He took a knife from his supply packet and sliced the rope off the girl's body. As he did so, Tanton spoke to her.

"I'm sorry to have treated you so roughly," he said, "but the act had to be convincing—for your sake as well as mine. What's your name, girl, and where are you from?"

For a moment she did not answer, her expression indicating extreme confusion. Then she whispered, "Glory Evans. I was captured in a raid on Smithton, Tennessee."

Speak up, girl," Tanton said in a not unkindly voice. "You're among friends now. You'll find clothing and safety down below."

Glory Evans did not react with any degree of gratitude. Instead, her fear deepened. Even on Earth she'd heard the horrors of the Undercity. To her, it seemed little different from the fate from which she'd been rescued.

"Things will be better now," Tanton assured her, "but we must keep moving. I'll lead the way. You, girl, walk behind me, and "Nine Successful Assignments" here, will cover the rear."

RON TOOK the sarcasm in silence and the three of them moved through the alley to stop at what appeared to be an abandoned plastic shack. Tanton tapped a code on the door panel.

While they waited. Ron wondered how the door, which opened outward, could be used before they moved the huge pile of refuse in front of it. He was soon to learn.

After a few minutes, during which time they had evidently been closely inspected from some hidden vantage point, the door opened. But it moved inward, frame and all, on hinges cleverly covered by strips of plastic. Tanton motioned and they climbed over the heap of debris into the small room beyond.

A wizened little Earthman was the keeper of this Undercity entrance. His mouth opened, revealing a toothless jaw, and he said, "You can go on down—on Margot's order, but I have no escort for you."

Tanton was relieved to hear the words, as he feared the order allowing his entrance into the Undercity accompanied by other persons had been cancelled. He'd told Margot he'd be back in three hours. It had been almost four months.

The old Earthman pushed back a panel in what seemed to be solid rock, and Tanton stepped through into a tunnel lit by a pair of dust covered levon tubes. When the girl hesitated, the blue Mercurian grasped her by the arm and pulled her through. His manner was not rough, but was far more firm than gentle, "We've no time to waste on timidity," he snapped.

Once beyond the panel, Tanton turned and, with a gesture, forbade the doorkeeper from closing it. "You'll have to go on alone," he said to Ron. "The two of you. I've got an appointment at the eighteenth hour that I've got to keep. I'll give you a note to Margot and a map showing how to get to her. Don't tell Margot you're an agent. I'll explain things in the note and she'll give you sanctuary."

Tanton wrote swiftly on a pad he took from his supply packet. Then he drew a map on another slip of paper and handed them both to Ron, "Things aren't tough enough as it is," he growled. "I've got to be saddled with a couple of babes in the wood on top of everything else."

Ron flushed. "See here—" he began.

"Obey orders," Tanton snapped. "Follow this map and you'll be all right." He went out through the panel as he'd come—then turned back. "And keep your zam-gun handy. You'll bump into some unsavory characters down there. A zam-gun speaks the only language they understand."

With that he was gone. The panel slammed, leaving Ron Kratnick and Glory Evans alone under a levon tube at the head of a long flight of stairs. Ron's resentment at Tanton's attitude was still in his voice as he said, "Well, we might as well get going." He resented being humiliated in front of this lovely girl, and unconsciously he took it out on her. "Give me your hand," he said. "I'll lead the way." Glory made no answer as—her hand tight in his—she followed Ron down the long flight of stairs.

At the foot of the stairs, they found a tunnel, lit at irregular intervals by levon tubes, stretching off into seeming infinity. The silence around them was like a live, sinister thing, waiting to pounce at the first opportunity. After traveling a hundred yards, Ron stopped and consulted Tanton's map. "It shouldn't be hard to find, but we've got to keep our eyes open. No telling what manner of creatures live in this cesspool."

AS THEY moved forward, the silence was broken, not by any abrupt sound, but slowly, imperceptibly, like leaves stirred by a breeze in a forest. Then gradually they could detect a new note that arose into a babble of sheer gibberish—the language and dialects of the Universe chuckling and babbling in the darkness.

The girl cringed against Ron. "I can feel them," she whispered in terror. "Eyes in the darkness, boring into me! What—what have we gotten into?"

"We've got to go on," Ron said, "It was Tanton's order, I have to obey."

"Will you make me a promise?" Glory Evans faltered. "Promise to kill me if—if—"

"It's not as bad as that," Ron answered. "These creatures down here know better than to face a zam-gun. They're probably just curious as to who we are."

Ron, entirely inexperienced so far as Venusia was concerned, listened to the gibberings and decided they were motivated by fear. Thus did he completely misinterpret the rising tone.

They were possessed of a diabolical cleverness, these obscene creatures—this legion of the damned lurking in the Undercity of Venusia. Clever to the extent that Ron and Glory were already identified as two inexperienced Earthlings; and also, word was being passed up and down the tunnels that Glory was an Earth girl, fair game for the lusts nurtured in unholy darkness. The word was being passed along, and now the tone of the chatterings was one of exultation.

Ron and Glory walked on, came to an indicated turn on Tanton's map, and moved into a new, broader tunnel.

Now, suddenly, there was complete silence, as though a

great hand had been clamped over the myriad mouths in the Undercity.

"See," Ron said. "They've stopped."

"Yes but why—why did they stop?" To the, terrified girl it was like a lull before some deadly storm.

"It's all right," Ron said. "Tell me what happened to you. You said you were taken in a raid?"

"Yes," Glory said. She was now walking close to Ron and, through sheer weariness, she no longer attempted to hide her lovely breasts from view. Worn and almost beaten, this futile attempt at modesty must have seemed a small thing to her, beside the horrors she had faced and was facing even now. Ron glanced down and his eyes caught the breathless contour of her young bosom and the smooth lines of her thighs and legs. He jerked his eyes guiltily away as she said, "It happened in the dead of night. We had guards in the town, but no one knew where the Venusians would strike next and it was impossible to cover every city and village. The space ship flashed down and those fiends were screaming in the streets and dragging people out of their homes before we knew what was happening. I was pulled from bed by a Martian raider and dragged from the house. On the porch I saw my mother lying dead—"

"Don't talk about it," Ron said quickly. "I'm sorry I brought it up." Then a trifle bitterly, "I seem to do the wrong thing and say the wrong thing with amazing regularity."

Glory Evans reached up impulsively and laid her hand on his chest. "Don't condemn yourself," she said. "It's all right. You've been good to me. I—I—you don't know what that means after what I've faced."

"I'll see that no one ever hurts you again," Ron said, warmly. "I'm going to—"

AT THAT exact moment, they were plunged into the middle of hell incarnate. From the balconies above, giving onto the tunnel, there poured a smothering army of pure horror out of dark crypts and passages.

In the light of the levon tubes Ron and Glory could see them, drooling, slithering, galloping, jumping from above—they came in such numbers as to make Ron's zam-gun useless.

Creatures from the Planetoids—some of which could have been classed as human and others undoubtedly lower animals—the products of places where evolution had run riot—had produced savagely and without regard to any known law.

Ron brought his zam-gun up and burned away three legs of a six-legged creature which had advanced upon him with a single great arm outstretched. A bat-like entity with the face of an Earthman and wings, spawned on some Planetoid, came hissing down from above. Ron cut it in two. It fell with a screech of agony and then Ron's gun was knocked from his hand. He saw a giant Plutonian reach out and pull Glory from a pile of furry, gibbering man-apes. But he could do nothing for her. He was held helpless in the iron grip of a shell-covered creature he couldn't classify.

He heard Glory scream once in terror. Then he went down into feathery darkness, spinning—spinning—spinning, as a great weight crashed against his skull.

CHAPTER FIVE

AFTER ridding himself of Ron and Glory, Tanton went cautiously back into the first tier of Venusia. The going was easier now because night had fallen and he had the advantageous cover of darkness.

He left the alley at its far end and found himself in a deserted street some two miles from the intersection of Darrien Promenade and Antor Street. It was well into the sixteenth hour and Tanton covered the two miles by the process of flitting from one shadow to another, avoiding the main thoroughfares with their bright levon tubes for the dim residential ways.

Upon arriving in the vicinity of the Promenade and Antor, Tanton veered to the left and found an alley leading him along one side of a giant warehouse. It was not by chance that he'd selected the particular intersection for his meeting with Valcan. He knew this neighborhood well, as was proven by the manner in which he found the small, ground level window into the warehouse.

Once inside, he lay hidden in a fuel bin until the watchman plodded past on his hourly rounds. Then Tanton commandeered an empty lift and rode to the forty-second floor. Quitting the lift, he let himself out on the roof and walked half a mile through a maze of ventilators until he came to the far side of the building. Time had moved halfway through the seventeenth hour.

Now, from his vantagepoint at the roof edge, he could look straight down upon the intersection at which he was to meet Valcan.

A scene of great activity was laid out below him. The

section had been roped off and, under strong lights, a great many men were working feverishly. They were operating in crews, digging into every nook, every suspicious corner which might house a hidden door into the Undercity. Brit-guns had been brought into play in order to cut passages through rock. Every door in the vicinity had been broken open and even sections of the pavement had been eaten away by the Brit-rays.

Tanton did not even bother to congratulate himself upon finding he had forecasted Valcan's move successfully. There had been no doubt whatever in his mind as to how the Secret Service Chief would proceed.

The man wanted, above all, a safe entrance into the Undercity. The cunning with which these entrances were hidden, had been the main thorn in Darrien's side. False entrances had been found from time to time, but they had invariably turned out to be death traps for Darrien's men. And upon the two occasions when true entrances had been found, it was almost as though Tza-Necros had given out the information himself, because the Undercity King's men were waiting for the onslaught of Darrien's warriors. And in each case after the slaughter, the entrance and dozens of the tunnels lying beneath, were sealed solid with ray-contaminated rock, which made sure death was the price of further tampering.

Tanton chuckled to himself at the sight of Valcan himself pacing restlessly about down below, receiving negative reports from his squads and venting his rage by smashing one lieutenant to the ground with a single blow of his fist.

TANTON waited patiently and, as the eighteenth hour approached, he saw Valcan call his men in and send them away, a group at a time until the area was practically deserted. The portable lights were extinguished and dragged away and finally, only Valcan himself remained, almost invisible now, in the deep shadow of a doorway.

Apparently satisfied, Tanton left the building by the same route he'd entered it. He emerged from the alleyway and leaned casually against a wall on Antor Street, scanning the passers-by. There weren't many. After a few minutes, Tanton selected a child of not more than ten years, collared him and pulled him close to the wall. He pointed down the street toward the doorway in which Valcan lurked.

"You see that entrance?" he said to the startled child. "You'll find a man standing there." Tanton thrust a folded piece of paper into the child's hand together with a ten-creda piece. "Carry this note to him and then be on your way. He won't hurt you. Just hand him the note and then go and spend these credas."

Released, the child was off at a dead run. Tanton watched as Valcan's arm came out of the shadows to take the proffered note. He imagined the reaction in Valcan's not-too-clever mind as he read:

Now that you've enjoyed yourself, let's go on with our business. Walk seven sectors down Antor street. If you have men following you I'll know it. If you try any tricks I'll probably have a chance to kill you.
Tanton

The blue Mercurian watched as Valcan wadded up the note and threw it angrily to the pavement, then looked searchingly up and down the street. Tanton could see the indecision working in Valcan's mind and was somewhat relieved when the latter finally quitted the doorway and strode down Antor Street with all the mannerisms of a sulky child.

Tanton did not follow Valcan. Instead he traveled swiftly up into the second tier of the thoroughfare and moved with long strides toward the rendezvous. His pace was such that, when Valcan had finished counting off seven sectors, Tanton's voice greeted him from a dark areaway:

"I'm glad to see you've come to your senses. Here—let me put this blindfold on you."

Valcan scowled and raised his hands in objection, whereupon Tanton said, "Don't be a fool. This alone should convince you I'm sincere. If you were allowed to find an entrance into the Undercity, you know very well Tza-Necros would never let you return alive."

The Secret Service chief made no further objection, allowing himself to be blindfolded and led back through the areaway by the crafty Tanton.

There followed now a period of what seemed aimless wandering. In truth it was just that, and eventually, Tanton brought Valcan back to the exact spot from which they'd departed. It was the place of his first entrance into the Undercity four months previous.

There was the red, peering eye, and once inside the plea: "A creda for food, my master. This miserable one starves while serving the great Tza-Necros."

Tanton knew the wretch was well fed and that the money would go for a brief hour of drug-induced ecstasy. He parted with a silver creda and led Valcan through the inner door and down into the first tunnel.

THERE he removed the blindfold. Valcan rubbed his eyes and scowled down the long passageway, "If I could bring Darrien information about this place—information with which to destroy it—I would soon sit far higher in his counsels," Valcan said.

And in Tanton's mind was a brusque, unuttered question: Doesn't this fool know he's going to die? How can a man allow lust of a woman and greed for prestige blind him to stark fact? How can men be so gullible?

"The vilest rats are the hardest to kill," Tanton said, easily, "But now we must hurry. And keep your gun handy. We may encounter resistance."

But there was no resistance—only eyes gleaming in dark places and the foul gibberings of creatures who had not seen sunlight for countless years.

Tanton left the Secret Service chief in the small anteroom to Margot's garden—left him under the watchful eye of the hostile young Plutonian—and hurried on to find Margot.

She was resting on a fur-covered lounge in her apartments. As Tanton entered, she arose and drew a robe around her golden body. "I thought you'd been killed," she said, and Tanton was elated to detect genuine concern in her eyes.

"It took longer than I thought," Tanton replied, "But nothing has changed. Aside from the time I spent in jail, the thing has gone off without a hitch." He hesitated for a moment. "You haven't changed your mind have you?"

She came toward him, a tired smile on her face, "If you had returned in three hours you'd have found me in a different mind. But for three months I've dreamed of freedom—of the good green Earth—and now—well, I'll do anything—anything to get away from this place."

"Excellent. Let me brief you on what is to be done." Seated beside Margot on the luxurious couch, Tanton explained very carefully what her role was to be, "And now I'll bring the fool in," he said. "Then I must seek an audience with Tza-Necros."

At the door, he turned back. "By the way, what have you done with my two babes-in-the-woods? You've put them out of harm's way I hope?"

Margot questioned with her eyes.

"Your babes-in-the-woods? What are you talking about?"

"An Earthman and a girl I took with me when I broke out of jail. I sent them to you with a note? You mean they didn't get here?"

"Of course not. I would have been told immediately."

The news saddened Tanton somewhat, but not too much. Obviously the two had been trapped—set upon out in the tunnels. By all odds they were dead now. Too bad. The girl was a raving beauty and the young agent was probably not beyond hope. He'd have probably been a good spy with a little guidance.

But, so long as neither of the two had been included in Tanton's original orders, he felt no responsibility for them. There were far larger things at stake than those two. With no further thought on the matter, he hurried across the garden to where Valcan was impatiently waiting.

"She is awaiting you," Tanton said. "And I must say, you are indeed a fortunate man. I regret that my own luck never exerts itself to such an extent in my behalf."

Valcan wore his perpetual frown. "Let's get ahead with it. This place makes me nervous. I wish now I'd signed that execution order."

"You'll change your mind when you see her," Tanton replied cheerfully.

He pushed Valcan through the inner door and closed it behind them, "This way," he said, and led Valcan down the yellow brick path.

"I can't believe it!" Valcan exclaimed. "I don't understand how such a place could have been built. It's beyond conception!"

"Slave labor," Tanton said, as if that explained the whole thing. "Margot is waiting over there. Come."

HE PUSHED Valcan into Margot's chamber, and when the latter saw Margot, reclining on the lounge, he stopped with a quick breath standing before her.

"Here is your new master, my dear," Tanton said.

Margot arose from the couch. "My lord," she murmured, and came forward, sensuous, languorous, her arms reaching.

Valcan took a step forward, but was brought to a halt by Tanton's sharp words. "Just a minute. There is a small formality before I can leave you to your own devices."

"I don't understand," Valcan said.

"I can understand why it slipped your mind—the matter of the projector's location. I have demonstrated my good faith and that of Tza-Necros by bringing you here. The time has come for you to deliver. Where is the projector located?"

Valcan's bedazzled mind was upon other things. Without taking his eyes from Margot's lush body, he said, "It is in a gray stone building on Neptune Way near the intersection of South Plaza. The building is marked as a food processing plant—"

Valcan brought himself up sharply upon the sudden realization of what he'd done. He'd told the truth! This crafty Mercurian had manipulated him into a trap. With devilish cunning, he'd asked his question at exactly the right moment—when Valcan's guard was down.

Valcan had told the truth and he was certain that Tanton knew it.

In so doing, Valcan realized he'd divested himself of his one weapon—his sole means of defense now that he had walked blindly into what could be a trap.

Swiftly his suspicions returned to be resolved into dreadful certainties. The blue Mercurian was no emissary of Tza-Necros! He was an agent of Earth Intelligence, sent to locate and destroy the ray projector. And—in league with this golden creature of the Undercity, he'd drawn information from Valcan which no method of torture, however fiendish, would have produced.

How could I have been such a fool? Valcan asked himself. His eyes darted, in desperation, toward the harness that lay on the floor near Margot's couch.

But he was never to get his hands on the zam-gun holstered in the harness. Margot, schooled by Tanton for just such a possibility as this, moved with swift grace to stoop and snatch the gun from its clip. She stepped backward, the gun ready for use, but her face showed both indecision and anger.

The latter was directed at Tanton, not Valcan, and her red lips framed an accusation. "You used me!" She said. "This talk about a ray projector. I don't understand it, but I know there is something wrong. What sort of an intrigue is this, Tanton?"

Her sudden perception threw the blue Mercurian slightly off balance. He hadn't expected it at this point.

A MOMENT later he was fighting for his life as Valcan hurled himself across the intervening space and smashed the agent to the floor.

"You'll never use that information!" Valcan yelled. He locked Tanton's arms to his side, thus preventing him from drawing his gun, and then wrapped his free arm around Tanton's head seeking to twist it from the agent's body.

Tanton managed to free his left arm as pain shot down his spine. He locked his hard, shell-covered hand around Valcan's throat and heaved upward with his knees. Valcan flew through space, but unfortunately for Tanton, his own zam-gun, knocked from its clip on his harness, bounced away also and skidded well beyond reach.

Both antagonists dived for the weapon. Both laid a hand on it at once. Then Margot's voice, so filled with fright and anguish as to freeze them both, cried out.

"Stop it! For God's sake, stop it!"

They, too, had heard the heavy footsteps coming in from the garden through the open portal. As one man, they turned and stared at what approached.

A great hairy monstrosity with the body of a giant ape, yet more erect and with a certain dignity in its movement. Two pairs of long arms extended from the thick torso upon which sat the ugly head of a Planetoid misfit. Only the eyes of the creature commanded respect. They were large, liquid, beautiful, perpetually brilliant. And without doubt they mirrored the able brain within the skull of Tza-Necros.

He was accompanied by a guard of four Plutonians, each armed with two zam-guns and a Brit projector.

Both Tanton and Valcan got slowly to their feet, their personal differences forgotten at the approach of this greater peril.

"He'll kill us all," Margot whispered in terror. "He'll kill us all."

Tanton looked desperately around for a means of exit. There was none. He lashed at his brain, demanding a plan of escape. But even Tanton's agile mind could not work miracles. It seemed his clever intrigue was to go for naught.

There's always some little angle you can't figure, he told himself sourly as Tza-Necros' gross body appeared in the doorway.

CHAPTER SIX

WHEN RON KRATNICK opened his eyes he was still not sure of having returned to consciousness. Truly the scene around him could as easily have been something in a nightmare. It was unbelievable.

He lay in what appeared to be a vast cavern. An open fire in its center threw weird dancing shadows on the faraway ceiling and walls. The fire also revealed a circle of bodies and faces. Hideous bodies and faces which could have well been done by a painter gone mad. Crouching, lascivious, blood-lusting entities formed a circle, well back from the fire, and there was continuous, terrifying sound as they jabbered, cackled and snarled in a hundred languages and dialects.

Close beside Ron lay the still body of Glory Evans. Her lovely back was curved as—with her knees drawn up—she buried her face in her arms. Ron slid a hand to her shoulder. She quivered from head to foot and Ron felt a sob run through her body.

Immediately the jabbering heightened as a thousand eyes saw that movement, and a giant voice roared out: "Be still, all of you! Stop this babbling or I'll lash the hides off you!"

Ron turned his head to behold an Earthman standing close to the fire. He was a giant in stature, close to seven feet in height. He wore a pair of tattered pants, sawed off just above the knees. His feet were naked and his great chest was covered with thick curly hair.

But it was the man's face that held Ron. A face mirroring a thousand years of evil. It had been slashed and scarred in a hundred brawls but—oddly—the monster's teeth were all in place—large, even, and white as Earth snow.

The man held a zam-gun in one hand and a long black whip in the other, and his manner left little doubt that he was commanding the situation. Ron lay motionless.

The man's voice boomed out, "We've had a piece of luck thrown our way and you fools are too stupid to realize it. I don't know if this man is worth anything, but the girl is a prize indeed."

And a chorus went up from the shadows to show that all the fiends agreed. "Graaaaa—yaoooo—fffffttaaaa!" and a sound like sharp teeth cracking bones.

The giant cracked his whip. "Silence! Listen to me! Listen to Caliban who can tear you apart a dozen at a time. Does anyone doubt that?"

The clamor subsided into a surly backwash and the one who called himself Caliban went on. "The trouble here is that none of you are equipped to think. The girl is a prize, yes, but what good is one girl when there are hundreds of us. We could only fight over her and many would be killed and the girl torn to pieces in the bargain."

Somewhere back in the shadows was an articulate voice, "Then let's start tearing. I'll take an arm to put around my neck when I go to sleep."

Another voice: "I'll take—"

But coarse laughter drowned out the rest and Caliban was shouting again. "We know that Tza-Necros has an eye for beauty. We know that had he seen this girl first, she'd never have come our way."

A shout of agreement.

"Then by all that's holy—let's sell her to him. If I'm any judge, Tza-Necros will pay us enough so that each man in the Undercity gets ten credas. Isn't that better than maybe a shred of flesh and probably nothing at all?"

THERE WAS a change in the gibbering and cackling.

The air was filled with whisperings now and many little conferences went on out in the darkness.

"If you agree," Caliban shouted, "I'll arrange a meeting with Tza-Necros and I promise you I won't come back empty handed."

A shout of approval went up. Immediately Caliban turned and prodded Ron with his foot. Ron came to a sitting position and Caliban bent down to sweep Glory Evans up into his arms.

"I'll put them in the prison," Caliban said, "and then negotiate with the Overlord."

Two willing lieutenants seized Ron by either arm and dragged him along in the wake of the striding Caliban. The circle broke at one side of the cavern and the place was quitted for a low-ceilinged tunnel leading off at a slightly rising angle. Some few hundred yards of this and another cavern was achieved, a smaller one but still large enough to house a small stone building with room to spare.

Two guardsmen stood in front of the door but their attitude, far from hostile, was almost ingratiating as Caliban said, "We have two tenants for you. We want to leave them here while I seek an audience with the Overlord."

The eyes of both guardsmen were on the body of Glory as Caliban cradled her in his arms like a child.

"You're going to sell her?" one of the guards asked.

"If Tza-Necros will buy."

"I'll buy," said the other, "I'll give you a hundred credas—platinum."

A roar of laughter went up from the citizens of the Undercity who were now pouring into the cavern, "Come back when you have a hundred thousand credas to spend," Caliban said. "Open the door."

The guard did as he was bidden and Caliban strode into the building and laid Glory on the floor. The jail was apparently a one-room affair occupying the entire building. It was very dark inside, the only illumination coming from the levon tubes outside the small windows.

Ron was shoved inside with such force that he went to his knees. He heard the door slam and the key turn in the lock. Then Caliban's booming voice directed, evidently, at the guards:

"You're going to be watched pretty closely while I'm gone, so I'd advise you to keep the door locked and stay outside."

A roar of understanding went up from the crowd. Quite obviously, the guards would not be left to themselves. Then Caliban's heavy footsteps faded away.

Ron got painfully to his feet and went to Glory Evans, who lay motionless on the floor. He knelt beside her and turned her so he could look down into her face. By the light of the levon tube rays filtering in, he could see the thick-lashed eyes open. His hand, having dropped unconsciously to her breast felt the rise and fall of her breathing. He snatched it away instantly. Somehow it seemed like taking advantage of helplessness.

Glory did not draw back from Ron's touch. In fact she did not seem conscious of it so much as the compassion in his attitude.

With sudden abandon and with a flood of tears, she threw herself into his arms and her manner was that of a child, a child searching for pity, tenderness, for something to keep from cracking up completely.

RON HELD her close in his arms as the explosion of tears and grief wracked her body. He said nothing, allowing her to cry herself out. And he was mute for another reason: he could think of nothing to say—no words of comfort for this harassed and tortured girl. There was only hopelessness, evil, and viciousness to be anticipated. Better that he remain silent.

He became conscious, now for the first time, of what Glory Evans really was. With her beauty held close in his arms, the perfume of her in his nostrils, he realized it had been more than a breaking point that had made him leap to her aid there by the cafe. He'd heard, vaguely, that sometimes love is like that, it can come suddenly, without apparent reason, and not even be recognized for what it is.

She was quiet now. She raised her face to his and he could see her smile in the dimness. "I'm sorry," she said. "Sorry for being such a problem to you. You've trouble enough without a weeping female on your hands."

Without thought, as naturally as taking a breath, Ron pulled her close and kissed her. An odd, tingling shock went through him at contact with her lips. She did not draw away. For a long moment she lay motionless, neither giving nor taking. Then she came alive with a suddenness that thrilled Ron and she accepted his kiss avidly, hungrily.

After an eternity, she drew away and nestled down into his arms. For a long time nothing was said. Then Ron's bitterness of spirit returned.

"I've failed you," he said miserably.

"Failed me? Don't say that. You've done your best. It will be easier—whatever comes will be easier—knowing this—having felt your arms around me—your kiss."

"I'm no good to you. Sure—I'm rated as a successful agent on Earth—nine assignments, but what were they? Local disturbances—things petty and unimportant beside an interplanetary project like this."

"You're wrong," she said, fiercely. "They wouldn't have sent you if they hadn't—"

"They sent me because they had no one else! It was a move of desperation. Why, I'm not in the same league with men like Tanton. It's like comparing an advanced scientist and a—a school boy!"

She put her fingers over his lips. "I won't let you say such things!"

But he drew her hand away and there was sudden hope in his face. "Tanton. I'd forgotten. Why, we aren't lost! Far from it. With Tanton calling the turns, it's just a matter of time. He'll get us out. Good old Tanton. He'll see that I get a chance to at least use my muscles even if I don't know how to use my head."

There had been faint sounds as of movement somewhere in the cell, but so intent had they been upon themselves, they hadn't noticed them. Now the sounds came louder, hoarse breathing and the shifting of a body.

Ron tensed as he searched the shadows about him. "Did you hear that?"

Glory raised fearful eyes. "Yes. There's someone else in this cell."

"A rodent of some sort maybe. I'll look around." He got slowly to his feet and sought to disengage himself from Glory, but she clung to him desperately.

"Don't leave me," she said. "I'll go with you. Let me hold your hand."

Together they moved softly in the direction from which the sounds came. The cell was a large one, running at least a hundred feet from wall to wall. It seemed miles until they finally caught sight of the figure lying prone in one corner.

"It's—it's a man," Glory whispered. "Another prisoner. It's—a blue Mercurian!"

Ron bent swiftly down over the figure. His hands explored. Then he braced himself and pulled the inert body forward into the dim light sifting through the window.

"It's *Tanton!*" he exclaimed in sheer unbelief.

CHAPTER SEVEN

AFTER leaving the jail cavern, Caliban threaded his way unerringly through the tunnels until he came to a great bronze door over which glowed several oversized levon tubes. He lifted in both hands the great iron knocker and allowed it to drop three times against the door. Three claps of thunder boomed through the tunnels. A full five minutes passed, after which a small door cut in the great bronze barrier opened to reveal two repulsive creatures of the Planetoids standing alert with drawn guns.

The giant eyed them with a certain contempt as he folded his great arms and said, "I am Caliban. The Overlord knows me well from keeping the rats in check down here. Tell him Caliban brings good news and would have an audience."

One of the guards stepped through the doorway to make sure Caliban was alone. Then he motioned the man inside and closed the door that Tza-Necros kept between himself and the scum roaming the tunnels of the Undercity.

One of the guards remained at his post while the other led Caliban through a maze of marble corridors to another closed door. Bidding Caliban to wait, the guard opened the door and stepped through, closing it after him.

But during that brief moment, Caliban's ears were struck by the surge of sound—the withering blasphemies roared out in a voice which would have put a bull to shame, the curses and oaths of ten planets spewing forth from the foul throat of a man beside himself with rage.

Caliban frowned. He knew that voice well. Tza-Necros was in a vile humor, to say the least. Caliban's annoyance at this turn of events was plain to see. He cared not a whit as to the luckless victim of Tza-Necros wrath. The thought in his mind was that the Overlord would be in no mood to do business.

When contented in mind, Tza-Necros would not hesitate to pay a hundred thousand credas for so lush an object of his lust as the fair-skinned Earth girl. This Caliban knew. But, in his present mood, Tza-Necros was unpredictable. He might even go so far as to have Caliban slaughtered in his tracks for no reason at all.

Frowning, the giant Undercity leader turned away from the door and began retracing his steps. He would return to the tunnels and wait for the storm to blow over.

But he had gone scarcely ten steps when the door opened and the guard called out. "Wait there! Where are you going? Tza-Necros commands your presence in the throne room."

Reluctantly Caliban turned back, cursing himself for a laggard and consigning his soul to the devils of Neptune. He marched into the throne room with his head held high, expecting the worst.

As the door closed upon him he stood transfixed at the sight he beheld. Tza-Necros, his four fists doubled and his arms held in rage above his ugly head, was standing on the dais in the center of the great room. On either side of him a line of frozen-faced guards were at motionless attention, their eyes staring straight ahead.

On the floor before the dais, lay a naked, golden girl of breathless beauty, a beauty that could be seen even through the blood she had shed and the torturous lashings to which she had been subjected.

AS CALIBAN entered the room, the whipmaster, a brawny Martian hillman, had stepped back and was running the whip through his closed hand to cleanse it of blood.

And Caliban could see the blood had not all been that of

the girl. Nearby lay the still body of an Earthman, and Caliban was startled to note that the official harness of Darrien's Secret Service on the back of the prone figure. A quick glance told Caliban the man had been beaten to death. The girl, however, was alive.

As Caliban entered the room, Tza-Necros beckoned with two arms and shouted. "Come forward, Caliban. You arrive at an opportune time, I have a present for you and your underground scum!"

"A present, my lord?"

"A rare one. This unfaithful witch is gall to my eyes. Entertaining lovers under my very nose. Betraying me after I've laid the treasure of the Universe at her feet. At first I thought it would sooth me to see the vile little wench flogged to death, but that is not enough and your coming has given me a happy thought."

"I am yours to command, my lord."

"Then take her down into the tunnels with you and sate yourself as only a bucko like you would know how to do."

"I can only consider myself fortunate."

Tza-Necros raised a hand. "That is not all. A stipulation, my faithful rogue. When you are through with her, I command you to seek out the most loathsome of your creatures and devise further tortures. And let the vengeance of Tza-Necros be seen by all. Take her."

Caliban stepped forward and lifted the unconscious Margot to his shoulder, "Thank you, my lord," he said, and turned to leave the throne room.

But he was brought to a halt by Tza-Necros' voice. The Overlord, now somewhat exhausted by his rage, was passing a hand across his forehead, "Hold until I release you," he said. Then in a milder, but petulant voice, "There was something. All devils I but with all this chatter about rays to clean out the Undercity and rays to hold off the Earthlings

72

and Margot consorting with two lovers at once—I can't get my thoughts straight. But there was something."

There was a moment of dead silence, after which Tza-Necros said, "Oh yes of course—your business. You did not wander in here by chance. What brings you up from the lower tunnels? Is there trouble—unrest?"

"No, my lord, I had business but it is of a trivial nature. I wouldn't think of bothering you with it at a time like this when you are wrought up by ingratitudes. It can wait."

"Good man, my Caliban. Come tomorrow and I'll have a flacon of wine for you."

Caliban went out as he had come and he was greeted in open-mouthed wonder by the guards. Old in experience, this was the first time they'd seen a man make his exit carrying a beautiful blood-soaked girl over his shoulder. They closed the door on Caliban and stood babbling between themselves.

Caliban was not happy. Far from satisfied with events, he went slowly down the tunnel, scarcely conscious of the girl he carried. What, he wondered, was all this talk about a ray to depopulate the Undercity. As to the troubles between Earth and Venus, Caliban cared nothing. He was content in the Undercity and that was where his loyalty and his interests lay.

He mulled over the snatches of information Tza-Necros had given out in his tirade and found them to be no information at all. Obviously the girl on Caliban's shoulder had been untrue to Tza-Necros, and for that Caliban hardly blamed her. But had a portion of Tza-Necros' wrath been generated by treachery of another nature? Who had that Earthman been—the one dead on the floor of the throne room? Obviously an official in the Secret Service.

Caliban shook his head in perplexity and went on his way.

CHAPTER EIGHT

TANTON was in deplorable shape. Obviously, he'd borne the brunt of a vicious attack during which weapons far more destructive than whips had been used. The hard shell covering found on all blue Mercurians in lieu of skin had been cracked in three places. The green life-sap that flowed in his veins had run freely from these wounds and from his nose and mouth.

As Ron pulled him into the light, Tanton opened his eyes and sighed deeply. "It was a great show while it lasted," he said in a labored voice, "I did some fast talking, but Tza-Necros went completely bats and refused to believe anything. Valcan was killed and maybe Margot too, for all I know. Mercurians are a lot harder to kill so I'm being saved for the hot hooks and the roasting pits."

He raised a hand to his battered head and then noted the consternation and bewilderment of Ron and Glory.

"You don't have the least idea what I'm talking about, do you? Well—it doesn't make any difference. By the way, what happened to you two?"

In a few words Ron told him, whereupon Tanton sighed again. "Couldn't even walk down a tunnel without getting into trouble, eh? Well, it doesn't matter. We'll all be buttoned up in twenty-four hours. It looks as though this one certainly backfired on me," He came to a sitting position, "Ouch! One of those guards used an iron club."

"You—you mean there's no hope?" Glory faltered.

"We're both sitting in the same spot," Tanton answered tartly. "Can you see any?"

His sharp mood was generated, not by fear of what

seemed the inevitable, but by the knowledge that he was being shown up as a failure before these two. "Help me to my feet, will you? I want to see how bad a shape I'm in."

As Tanton creaked and twisted erect, the sounds outside the prison deepened into a roar. "Something's going on," Ron said, "Maybe they're coming for us." He turned to face the door, his arm around Glory's slim shoulder.

The door opened after some minutes of heated controversy outside, and Caliban strode in with Margot over his shoulder. Tanton's eyes widened. Without preliminaries, he asked, "Where did you get her?"

"A gift to the citizens of the Undercity by Tza-Necros," Caliban said. He was frowning and seemed bemused—far away—as though deep in thought. "I'm going to put her away until I can figure this thing out. There's more here than meets the eye. Tza-Necros says she wasn't faithful to him, but there's more—a lot more—and I don't like it."

No one saw Tanton's eyes brighten as he watched Caliban place Margot on the hard floor. And it was of course impossible for the rest of them to know what was going on in his rapier sharp mind—that he was even now formulating plans to turn defeat into victory.

GLORY, WITH a cry of pity, dropped to her knees beside the still Margot and cradled the golden beauty's head in her lap.

Tanton ignored both of them, his eyes on Caliban, "I don't think I've had the pleasure," he said.

The other scowled at him, "My name is Caliban, I've lived in the Undercity for twenty years. Who are you and where do you come from?"

Ron opened his mouth to fill in with an introduction of his superior, but a quick motion of Tanton's hand blocked off the young agent's words.

"I am a gentleman of fortune," Tanton replied and there was a distinct note of sadness in his voice. "I garner information and go about selling it, making a creda wherever possible. But now I've come to the end of my string."

There was contempt in Caliban's voice. "Oh—an informer. And Tza-Necros has condemned you to death?"

Tanton sighed as if in resignation, "True, but I will not suffer in the roasting pit. I'll die here in this hole along with the rest of the Undercity's people. In twenty-four hours there won't be a single living thing below ground in Venusia."

Caliban snatched the bait and bolted it down—swallowed it whole. He advanced menacingly upon Tanton. "What are you talking about, Blue man. Is it something about a ray that will destroy all life in the Undercity?"

Tanton was taken aback—at least his wide eyes so indicated. "You seem to know a great deal, Caliban. May I ask—?"

The huge Earthman frowned importantly, "I have my sources of information. I have ears and eyes."

Tanton made as if to turn away. "Then there is nothing I can tell you, except that I think we should both do the merciful thing."

"What do you mean?"

"Keep our knowledge to ourselves. It will do no good to panic the Undercity by telling the people the truth. So long as they must die, let them die quietly without knowing what hit them."

Caliban strode forward and seized Tanton roughly by the shoulder, "You mean we should lie here like rats in a trap waiting for death?"

"What else is there to do?"

Caliban brushed aside all pretense. "You know far more than I—tell me."

Tanton nursed his cracked shoulder-shell. "There isn't a

great deal to it. You know, of course, that Darrien swore long ago to clean out the Undercity. But it was only recently that he found a means of doing so—a poison ray which will be turned into an entrance to the Undercity—an entrance which his men have found—a ray which will travel into every nook and cranny of this place and not even the smallest microbe will be left alive, I tell you when Darrien gets through, the Undercity will be the most sterile place in the Universe."

"How do you know all this?"

"Getting such information is my business. In this case I corrupted a high official of Darrien's Secret Police—promised him great wealth when Tza-Necros heard his story. The man I brought into the Undercity was the Secret Service chief himself—Valcan."

Caliban clenched his great fist. Of course! The Earthman he'd seen lying dead at Tza-Necros' feet. The face had seemed familiar. Now he knew! The man had been Valcan. "What happened?" Caliban demanded.

TANTON shrugged. "I made a mistake. I did not have direct access to Tza-Necros. I could reach his ear only through Margot, for whom I once did a service." Tanton stopped and shook his head sadly, "But such an approach was a fatal mistake, because Tza-Necros found us in Margot's apartment and accused us of being her lovers. We were dragged into the throne room and beaten. Valcan died under the lash and I'm to be roasted on hot hooks. But, as I say, that will never happen, because—"

Caliban waved an impatient hand, "Stop babbling," he shouted. "You said the ray will be used within twenty-four hours? Do you know the location of the projector?"

"Yes, but Tza-Necros would not listen—"

"The fool!" Caliban thundered, "The thick-headed fool!

Sacrificing the lives of all of us because of his stupidity."

"I'd hesitate to put it so bluntly, but that's about it. Well—no matter now. The game has been played and lost."

Caliban towered over the blue man and raised his fists, "What are you—a spineless jellyfish? Do you propose to cringe against the wall and wait for death?"

"What else is there to do?"

"Fight, man, fight! There are ten thousand creatures down here—ten thousand fighters who have groveled too long under the heel of Tza-Necros. With their lives at stake do you think they'll stand helplessly by?"

It was as if a great plan had suddenly blossomed in Tanton's mind. "Why, of course! Why didn't I think of it?" His eyes lit up with a great hope. "I can see it now. Ten thousand citizens of the Undercity streaming up into Venusia, not only to destroy the ray but to avenge a hundred years of persecution! It's—it's magnificent!"

Caliban strode to the door and threw it open. His great voice boomed out, echoing and reechoing through the tunnels: "Citizens of the Undercity. Hear me! Come and gather around if you value your lives! We have been betrayed and left to die! All of you who would strike a blow for your own existence, come and hear me!"

Inside, Tanton closed the door. Then he crossed to where Margot was regaining consciousness, and knelt beside her. "I'm going to keep my word," he said. "In a matter of hours you'll be on your way back to Earth. Things didn't go exactly as I'd planned, but—"

He stopped speaking as Glory, who was still cradling Margot, gave a low cry of wonder and horror. Ron also came close and knelt down. He raised his eyes to Tanton with a look of utter consternation, then lowered them again to where Margot was changing—magically—before their eyes. First, small wrinkles had appeared at the corners of her mouth and her eyes. Now the flesh—the glorious golden beauty of her was shrinking visibly—drying up and falling away under skin that was becoming gray and withered.

Margot's mouth—now an ancient and toothless one—opened like the mouth of a gasping fish.

"The hormones," she croaked. "I was supposed to take the hormones—I—"

The aging became swifter now. It was like some mad montage—a young and beautiful girl fading away and a hideous wrinkled crone taking her place.

"The hormones," she gasped. Then the pitiful old mouth opened and hung slack, the gray-coated, sightless eyes became set in a ghastly stare.

SWIFTLY, Tanton reached down and closed the eyes forever. "She was—very old, you know," he said quietly, "Well over a hundred years. She was kept young by a secret hormone that Tza-Necros provided. Without it, she was doomed."

"She's—she's *dead!*" Glory breathed in horror. So swift had been the transition from blooming beauty to dried-up skeleton, that the effect was chilling in its grimness.

Tanton lifted the wisp of a body and moved off into the shadows, "She lead a full life," he said, "A very long life. But I have a feeling she's happier now than she's ever been," He returned, empty-handed, to the wide-eyed Glory, "Maybe someone ought to say a prayer," he muttered, then turned toward the door as the voice of the mob outside rose to a thunder.

The door opened and Caliban rushed in. "We're on the move," he shouted. "If you know where the ray is located, you'd better lead the way."

But Tanton knew it was more than the nonexistent death ray that motivated this upheaval. His lie had been merely the trigger—the small thing that had touched off the revolt. True motivation lay far deeper. Here was an irresistible surge of outraged humanity—horrible humanity it was true, but humanity nonetheless—moving up in fury to right ancient wrongs.

And it was in Tanton's mind where the first seeds of this violence had been sewn—long ago by the pompous voice of a politician: (*"Let Venus be our penal colony—"*). And there must have been a twinge in the Blue Mercurian's conscience, because he told himself: One must weigh two evils and attack the greater with the smaller. All is greed and hunger among men and their greed and hunger are the only effective weapons to be used against them. To defeat darkness, the tools of darkness must be used.

Then the roar of the mob rose to an even greater volume to bring Tanton back to the business at hand.

CHAPTER NINE

GLORY HAD been provided with adequate clothing—the harness of a fighter—and she moved—with Tanton, Ron, and Caliban—at the head of a column that assaulted the bronze door to Tza-Necros' underground palace.

The door was cut to pieces and a wave of misfits of the Universe, swept over all resistance in its onward surge. Guarded by a circle of Undercity warriors, Glory saw Tza-Necros—his inner guard annihilated—battling like ten demons with his back to the wall.

The Undercity fighters lay in stacks around him. His more lethal weapons gone, he slashed a crimson circle with a short sword clutched in each of his four hands. "Back—back, you foul scum!" he roared. "I am your king! I am your master!" And he proved himself their master right up to the final, bloody moment when a zam-gun ray cut off his arms, one by one and left him a helpless, screaming maniac. The scum of the Universe moved in on him then, to take bloody accounting for the years of pain and exploitation. They gloried in tearing him to pieces, bit by bit—in inflicting savage torture until his last scream became a gurgle as life left his grotesque body. His last words were a bewildered plea: "I'm one of you—One of you—one of you. Have mercy."

Then death.

The mob, aflame from the new freedom and the smell of blood, surged on through the palace, tearing Margot's garden to pieces, brick by brick. Then up into Venusia, along with the hordes of fellow exiles that were streaming out of the Undercity entrances to spread bloody destruction in all directions.

The astonished population of Venusia stared in flat-footed horror at the sudden egress from the depths, many of them stared too long and went down to quick death as the waves of madness released, engulfed and destroyed them. The policing mechanisms of the city went into complete panic and chaos. The more experienced Secret Service and the City Police were unable to function because of the panicked populace. There was no room for maneuvering—no chance to assemble and deploy, so mad was the scene of carnage and so frenzied the attack.

Tanton, moving at the head of Caliban's column, adroitly held the latter to the main objective—the ray projector. Working through the giant Earthman, he displayed a skill that any great general would have envied. Truly, the man seemed possessed of limitless talents.

Due to his generalship, the column was organized and thrown around the gray building with military precision. The assault on the entrances was launched as one movement. The doors were beaten down and Glory, Ron, and Tanton, were among the first of the invaders to be swept inside.

Glory heard herself screaming, calling out to be heard over the din of battle. "Caliban! I saw him go down!"

"He was cut in two with a zam-gun," Tanton shouted. "Come—this way! Quick!" He pushed Glory roughly toward a stairway leading off in to upper levels, and motioned Ron to follow. There was deep concern in Tanton's voice because, again it seemed, ill luck was besetting him.

OUT IN THE streets there had been panic and chaos, but not so in the ray projector building. Here was the cream of Darrien's vanguards—the picked soldiery of the entire Universe—trained and briefed for only one job—the protection of the ray projector at any cost.

Their ranks had been dented by the first wave of crazed

Undercity fighters, but they had stiffened and gotten down to their work. Like machines, they poured death into the invaders—like implacable robots, they reformed their lines and hurled back Caliban's hordes. And in this action, Tanton sensed his own defeat.

He knew full well that the Undercity fighters would be beaten. When Darrien's organized ranks gained their footing they would move like a steamroller over the deceived and misled creatures from underground. Truly—though with much blood and rapine—it would be the end of the Undercity, but Tanton had gambled that, during the upheaval, he could accomplish his purpose. Now he seemed doomed to defeat, as the elite guard of the gray building pushed the last of Caliban's sorry army out into the streets and made fast their own defenses.

With the main action going on below, Tanton found no one to bar his way as he led the two Earthlings up the stairs. His hopes bloomed anew at the thought that possibly he could achieve his ends by stealth. The projector would certainly be located high up in the building. Maybe it could still be reached. Possibly even Darrien's elite guard had made the mistake of depending on the first line of defense down below and had given no thought to the danger of infiltration through their ranks.

The infiltration had been accomplished, and as the three invaders went higher and higher without encountering resistance, Tanton allowed himself to hope anew.

They reached the top abruptly, coming to the head of a staircase and finding themselves on a circular platform just under the roof of the building. The platform ran around a giant opening. A steel railing was built thereon to keep the unwary from tumbling down into a great pit twenty floors deep.

In the center of this pit lay Tanton's assignment, a

tremendous silvery ray-tube, anchored at the bottom and extending upward to almost the level of the platform. Laid out horizontal, the tube would have covered over an acre of ground, and from its curved, silvery top, an invisible ray could be heard as it went out through an opening in the roof to blanket Venusia and explode any missile moving in that direction.

Tanton could not smother the shout of triumph that welled up in his throat as he saw the pile of anti-gravity discs piled on one side of the platform. Certainly he could not have planned things better. Scanning the roof, he stepped to the wall and pushed a lever. Immediately another section of the ceiling drew back to make an opening large enough for comfortable exit. Evidently the platform was also used as a hangar for guards on sky patrol.

Tanton swiftly hauled three of the plates out onto the platform. From a pile lying near the wall, he tossed a pair each of gravity shoes to Ron and Glory.

"Put them on," he shouted, "Then get on the plate and wait for me above the building." As he spoke, he donned a pair of the shoes himself, "As soon as I give the signal," he said to Ron, "send word to the Earth squadron out in space that the ray is destroyed. And don't wait for me. After they get word we've got to get out of here quick or we'll be killed by falling bombs. This whole place is going up in atomic dust."

RON SHOWED Glory how to guide the anti-gravity plate by moving her body. Then he threw the switch and steered her through the roof opening. Swiftly, he set his shoes on his own plate and followed her.

It was after they had cleared the building and were hovering within sight of Tanton, that disaster struck. It came in the form of a dozen guards who had crept up the stairs and were advancing on Tanton from three directions. They came as silently as clouds because a quick glance at the situation had shown them their problem. The blue Mercurian was there of course to destroy the projector. Therefore they must get their hand on him rather than blast him down, because he stood so close to the edge of the platform that he could easily fall into the pit.

Tanton, intent upon his work, raised his head and saw the men creeping in—but too late. Turning in the heavy gravity shoes, he heard Ron's voice from above.

"Hold it!" Ron yelled. "I'm coming back to help!"'

In a matter of seconds, Tanton took in the situation, estimated his chances and made his decision, "Don't come back!" he yelled. "You can't help. Take the girl away and give out the signal! That's an order!"

Ron slanted his plate out of the dive and then, before his horrified eyes, Tanton made a last contribution toward the security of Earth.

Just as the hands of a guard reached out to seize him, he hurled the man backward with a single sweep of his arm and took a step forward. Held down by the heavy shoes, it was a slow step, but there was just time for another.

The second step was into space and Tanton went plunging down into the pit, smashing—with his own body—the great tube of the ray projector.

There was an explosion so loud and with such force, that it hurled Ron and Glory far up into the sky. When their anti-gravity plates steadied, Ron looked, grim-lipped, at the white-faced Glory—saw that she was unhurt—and pulled a small radio transmitter from his supply packet. He set the dial and a moment later his voice came in on the board of the *California Queen*, flagship of Earth's Space Fleet Three:

"Ronald Kratnick—Earth Intelligence to squadron commander. Umbrella destroyed. Umbrella destroyed."

Twice he sent the message before hearing the response, "Message received."

Ron didn't even bother to repocket his transmitter. He threw it from him and yelled to Glory: "Let's get out of here—and fast! Straight up!"

They reached the glass dome of Venusia in a matter of seconds and now, with the projector destroyed, they were able to go safely through the opening in the dome through which the protective ray had been allowed to escape.

On they went, ever upward until Ron tilted close to Glory's anti-gravity plate and—just to be on the safe side—clamped an oxygen cup over her nose. He had only one cup available, and when Venus was lost in the haze beneath them and the heat of the sun began breaking through the dark Venusian clouds, Ron began to feel a little lightheaded.

Moments later their spirits lifted as they saw the silver oval of the *California Queen* breaking through the clouds, with space-suited rescuers streaking toward them on anti-gravity discs. Both rescuers were female, their capes blowing in the wind. They pointed toward the ship and beckoned Ron and Glory to follow. How ironic, Ron thought, to be rescued by two lovely female space soldiers high above a planet where Earth women were held in such cheap regard.

As they streaked through the thin atmosphere toward the *California Queen*, the fleet's bombs smashed down on Venusia and left a great yawning hole in the red forests of the planet.

THE COMFORTS aboard the California Queen were such as to wipe away quickly, the horrors of the Undercity. Ron, seated in the lounge, holding Glory's hand, had been silent for some time. Glory looked up at him and smiled.

"I'm going to leave Intelligence," Ron said.

"That surprises me," Glory replied, "but I'm glad—very glad."

"It's because of *him*."

"I don't understand."

Ron smiled. There was a sadness in the smile. "It's hard to explain, but—well, he was a schemer, a liar, a master of intrigues and there was nothing he wouldn't do to gain his ends. But over and above it all, he was *great*—that's the only word I can think of to describe him. He was willing to give his life for any cause to which he pledged himself, and there is no sterner test of any man than that."

"And that's why you're resigning, darling?"

"No, it's because, after seeing him operate, I know I can never be better than second grade. I was a school child beside Tanton, and I won't be a second-grade anything. If I can't be the best, I'll drop out."

His smile deepened. "You know—I think I'd make a swell farmer. In fact I think I could be a farmer second to none."

After he'd kissed her, Glory said, "That's wonderful, darling. And I think I could be the best farmer's wife in the Universe."

THE END

If you've enjoyed this book, you will not want to miss these terrific titles...

ARMCHAIR SCI-FI & HORROR DOUBLE NOVELS, $12.95 each

D-21   **EMPIRE OF EVIL** by Robert Arnette
THE SIGN OF THE TIGER by Alan E. Nourse & J. A. Meyer

D-22   **OPERATION SQUARE PEG** by Frank Belknap Long
ENCHANTRESS OF VENUS by Leigh Brackett

D-23   **THE LIFE WATCH** by Lester Del Rey
CREATURES OF THE ABYSS by Murray Leinster

D-24   **LEGION OF LAZARUS** by Edmond Hamilton
STAR HUNTER by Andre Norton

D-25   **EMPIRE OF WOMEN** by John Fletcher
ONE OF OUR CITIES IS MISSING by Irving Cox

D-26   **THE WRONG SIDE OF PARADISE** by Raymond F. Jones
THE INVOLUNTARY IMMORTALS by Rog Phillips

D-27   **EARTH QUARTER** by Damon Knight
ENVOY TO NEW WORLDS by Keith Laumer

D-28   **SLAVES TO THE METAL HORDE** by Milton Lesser
HUNTERS OUT OF TIME by Joseph E. Kelleam

D-29   **RX JUPITER SAVE US** by Ward Moore
BEWARE THE USURPERS by Geoff St. Reynard

D-30   **SECRET OF THE SERPENT** by Don Wilcox
CRUSADE ACROSS THE VOID by Dwight V. Swain

ARMCHAIR SCIENCE FICTION CLASSICS, $12.95 each

C-7   **THE SHAVER MYSTERY, pt. 1**
by Richard S. Shaver

C-8   **THE SHAVER MYSTERY, pt. 2**
by Richard S. Shaver

C-9   **MURDER IN SPACE**
by David V. Reed

ARMCHAIR MASTERS OF SCIENCE FICTION SERIES, $16.95 each

M-3   **MASTERS OF SCIENCE FICTION, Vol. Three**
Robert Sheckley, "The Perfect Woman" and other stories

M-4   **MASTERS OF SCIENCE FICTION, Vol. Four**
Mack Reynolds, Part One, "Stowaway" and other stories

AN ALIEN ATTACK WAS IMMINENT...

It sounded unbelievable, but that's what the people of Earth were being told by the top brass at the Department of Internal Affairs; and strange incidents from all over the world seemed to confirm it. However, if there had been any doubters left to question the credibility of this fantastic story, their doubts were washed away one afternoon when Earth's lone satellite, the moon, exploded in the sky above. And soon the people of Earth braced themselves for the worst…

Veteran science fiction writers Alan E. Nourse and J. A. Meyer spin a taut tale of incredible intrigue and impending horror in this top-of-the-line novel from the golden age of fantastic literature—straight from the pages of Amazing Stories *magazine. "The Sign of the Tiger" is a remarkable science fiction gem.*

CAST OF CHARACTERS

HARVEY ALEXANDER
Not exactly a man of steel. But he was wise beyond his years—and amazingly adept at sidestepping destruction.

JULIAN BAHR
An ego-driven man without mercy. His ruthless ambitions seemed unstoppable and reached well beyond the stars.

LIBBY ALLISON
She was brilliant and she was beautiful. But her strange love for Bahr forced her into acts unspeakable.

CARL ENGLEHARDT
A king in the world of financiers. He used his wealth like a club—to knock over nations!

FRANK CARMINE
Loyal to Bahr in all things from meditation to murder. But he proved that even faithful dogs can sometimes go mad.

PAUL MACKENZIE
The silent Scot. He watched and waited and plotted to topple the Colossus who would rule the Earth.

BART ADAMS
A man of great resources who made poor use of his power. His hatred of Bahr had become an obsession.

THE SIGN OF
THE TIGER

By
ALAN E. NOURSE and J. A. MEYER

ARMCHAIR FICTION
PO Box 4369, Medford, Oregon   97501-0168

CHAPTER ONE
Bahr Moves In

THE alarm went off at ten minutes to midnight, splitting the drowsy silence of the Power Plant guardroom, jarring the two corporals into stunned wakefulness.

The duty Sergeant burst into the room. "Geiger alert!" he yelled. "For Pete's sake, don't just stand there, call the OD. Switch on the floods and the radar sweep…"

He snapped on the squawk box to the Plant Security Police barracks and turned up the volume. Behind him the corporals were frantically pulling emergency switches, flooding the whole rain-soaked compound of the Wildwood Slow-Neutron Power Plant with invisible infrared.

"Geiger alert," the Sergeant growled into the squawk box. "Get all your flying squads up. Burp guns, ground trucks and squooshers ready. Got that?"

"What happened? Where?" the voice came back.

"How do I know where? Somewhere in Sector Five…" The Sergeant checked the alarm tape. "…about five miles north of the gate. Somebody's gotten U-metal through the gate units. Send the ground trucks out on Road 423."

North of the Plant, the leading ground truck churned up the road.

"Light up ahead," the driver said suddenly, slamming the brake.

"Put the beam on them," the corporal said, cranking his burp gun and letting the safety lid snap open. "It may be what we're after." He stuck his head out of the cab, shouting back at the trucks behind. "SQUOOSHERS…READY!"

"Hold it," the driver said. "They're signaling back. It's a DIA field unit."

The corporal blinked. "DIA…what in the hell are they doing out here?" He stuck his head out again. "HOLD IT…HOLD IT…DIA UNIT."

The corporal stumbled out of the truck, shielding himself

against the rain, and started ahead toward the light. "What's a DIA unit doing here?" somebody mumbled behind him. "Those guys hit faster than strychnine. It's only been ten minutes since the alarm went off."

"Army?" a voice asked.

"That's right. 923rd Security Police, Wildwood Power Plant."

"All right, put those burp guns on safety," the voice said.

From the third truck back a Lieutenant came stamping up in the mud. "Corporal, why are we stopped? I didn't give any orders to stop here. Who are these men?"

"Carmine, DIA." The man pulled a badge out of his civilian raincoat pocket and flashed it briefly.

"Oh," the Lieutenant said, quieter. The corporal grinned.

Someone came out of the darkness, a big man in a belted black raincoat and plasti-covered hat. He had enormous shoulders and a heavy, powerful body, yet he had come down the road without a sound, like a tiger coming down to a watering place. "That Security?"

"That's right, Mr. Bahr," Carmine answered. The man called Bahr moved forward and squinted at the Lieutenant.

"I'm Julian Bahr...DIA. We picked up an alarm on our atomic net and got a field unit in here. Was that signal inbound or outbound?"

It caught Axtell unprepared. "I...don't know, sir."

"Then we'll assume it was outbound. U-metal theft," Bahr said. "Whoever it was can't have gotten far yet in this brush, and we know he's not on the road. I want you to deploy your men in a large circle around the strike point. Send your trucks out in a pincers and drop a man off every quarter mile with an eye-beam."

Down the road a siren whined. A winking red turret light was dodging swiftly up the road. Then the car, a sleek mud-spattered Volta 400 one-wheeler, ground to a halt a few yards from Bahr. A short, lean, rain-coated officer with Major's leaves on his shoulders was the only one in the car. He jumped out into the mud. "What's the holdup here?"

The Lieutenant saluted. "Sir…these DIA men told me…"

The Major looked from the Lieutenant to the DIA men and back. His face was gray and heavily lined, but his eyes were bright with anger. "DIA? What's the Department of Internal Affairs doing on a military security problem?"

"We picked up the alarm on our atomic net," Bahr said, moving forward. "We've been waiting here for over ten minutes," he added pointedly. "I directed your men here to circle the strike area and fence it in."

"On whose authority?"

"Atomic Security Act of 2005," Bahr said. "That was an outgoing signal from your road monitor. That means a theft of U-metal from your Plant until proven otherwise."

"You haven't been called in on the problem," the Major said.

Bahr snorted. "You were a little too late to call us in. We've already got roadblocks mounted. We had a 'copter unit in the air at the time of the alarm. We stationed it immediately." He hunched his shoulders forward, with a glance at Carmine. "Whoever broke U-metal out of the power plant has taken to the woods by now."

"Then I'll send a unit in after them," the Major snapped.

"In this downpour? You're fifteen minutes late for that. The only chance now is a circling move." Bahr started to move off down the road.

"Wait a minute. I'm Major Alexander, 923rd Security. These are my troops, my territory, and my problem. I don't want a lot of Washington Intelligence men nosing around this Power Plant."

The other spoke coldly. "My name is Bahr. Assistant Director, DIA." He flashed his badge and moved forward a step. "And I'd like to know what sort of a Security system you're running that lets hot stuff get five miles outside your compound before it's picked up by monitors."

Alexander felt a sudden knotting in his stomach. DIA meant investigation, a full DEPCO psych-probe, months of interrogation, stability downgrading…ruin. And DIA could play the sluggish arrival of his Security troops into anything they wanted. "Are you making this a straight DIA project?"

"I'm making it a joint maneuver," Bahr said. "My organization and your personnel. I'll have more DIA units here in fifteen minutes. In the meantime I don't want anybody or anything to get out of that strike area."

"All right," Alexander said, "then we'll combine efforts." He turned to Axtell. "Lieutenant, deploy your troops on Mr. Bahr's orders."

Axtell saluted.

Bahr turned on his heel and slogged across the road strip into the clearing where his 'copter had landed, Carmine at his side. Angrily, Major Alexander followed through the mud. A man was standing by the 'copter radio. "Have we got anything?" Bahr asked the radioman.

"Unit B just reported in, Mr. Bahr. Seven 'copters."

"Give them the strike point coordinates. Tell them to use an expanding square and drop their Geigers through the trees on cables at thirty-yard intervals." He turned to Alexander. "What we need to know now is how much U-metal was stolen. Do you know how much is missing from the Plant?"

"No U-metal is missing from the Plant," Alexander said tightly. "There are exit monitors at all the gates and none of them have recorded radioactives going out."

Bahr stared at him. "Are you trying to tell me that a road alarm goes off five miles from your plant indicating hot stuff being moved away from the pile, and yet nothing has disappeared out of the Plant?"

"I don't know what tripped the road Geiger," Alexander snapped. "All I know is that nothing could have been smuggled from the plant. Our Security system is quite thorough."

"Your Security system stinks," said Bahr. "Do you by any chance keep an inventory of the U-metal at the Plant?"

"Certainly," Alexander said, his face very red.

"Well, take another one right now. I want every slug of U-metal and every cubic inch of slush accounted for."

"You're out of your mind," Alexander said. "All of greater St. Louis is using our heat and power. You can't just turn off a power plant the way you cut a station off the air."

Bahr grabbed up the radio mouthpiece. "Get me Unit C."

"Listen," Alexander burst out. "I warn you…"

"This is Bahr," the big man said into the mouthpiece. "There is a change of plan for Unit C. I want all personnel to land inside the compound at the Wildwood Plant. I said *inside*. I want a complete inventory on the U-metal in that plant. I want to know how much has been stolen, and I don't care how you find out."

"You have no authority inside that compound," Alexander said. "If your 'copters are fired on, it'll be your own responsibility. My men have orders…"

"They won't be fired on," Bahr cut him off. "Nobody fires on DIA 'copters."

Overhead, six fiery red circles made by jet-tipped 'copter blades were moving across the field toward a patch of woods, buzzing just over the treetops, hanging motionless as Geigers were dropped through the trees and then reeled up again, then moving on.

Bristling with rage, Alexander scuffed back through the mud to his Volta, turned on the sending unit, and contacted the relay back at the Plant. "This is Alexander. I want a crash priority through to Washington. Urgent, personal, to John McEwen, Director, DIA. Reference Wildwood Power Plant: *your assistant Bahr orders shutdown of entire project for investigation, stop, exceeding authority, stop, request you direct him to rescind this order pending further study and evidence, stop, Harvey Alexander, Major, nine-two-three Security, reply immediately. Out.*"

He knew the Security system at the Plant because he had personally organized it from top to bottom. After his downgrading from BURINF, when they had ordered him to the military limbo of this antique power pile in the Illinois flatlands, Harvey Alexander had realized that his only hope for reinstatement would be a record of exemplary execution of his new job, the Security protection of the Plant. Within a week he had studied and thrown out the old, ineffective Security system and installed his own.

It was as perfect a system as Alexander knew how to devise, and he was singularly expert on the matter of Security systems...though—beside himself—only God and BRINT knew that. And he knew that no U-metal could have left the Plant without his knowing it...

But even if it had, why the panic? Who would try to steal U-metal? It was as useless as gold bullion. There was no market for it. The Wildwood Plant was one of the oldest piles in existence, built in the twentieth century with all the engineering inefficiencies that the 1960's had produced. The U-metal slugs it used would only fit that particular pile. And what could there be about a U-metal theft...the most impractical of all crimes...that attracted the DIA?

The crackle of the radio jerked him back to alertness. "Major Alexander. ASPX nine-two-three calling Major Alexander."

He picked up the speaker, held the switch down. "Yes, here."

"Washington refers us to Lowrie Field, Denver, sir. McEwen is on vacation there."

"Then re-send the message," Alexander said. "Plain-language heading *Personal McEwen.'* Put it on a Q priority."

"Yes, sir."

He leaned back, sweat pouring down his sides. Everything now depended on McEwen backing him up. And that, he thought warmly, he could count on. McEwen had been doing that for twelve years.

For all the ominous reputation of investigations, arrests, and interrogations carried on by the Department of Internal Affairs...the dreaded civilian intelligence organization that served as watchdog for the new Vanner-Elling Stability government...one main fact had always remained paramount.

The DIA would never exceed the legal limits of its authority. Even Alexander, after his brief and bitter experience in the Bureau of Information, still believed this to be accurate.

He jumped as the door of the Volta slid open and Bahr stood there, rain pouring from his hat. "I need your car," he said. "A couple of our ground units have been flown in about a mile up the road, and I…"

The squawker boomed, "Strike! Mr. Bahr…there's a strong signal on a Geiger from Unit B 'copter Number Seven. They're holding position. Over."

Bahr picked up the speaker, rotated the broadcast selector to the DIA frequency. "This is Bahr. Number Seven? What have you got there?"

"Can't see it, but we get a hell of a jolt on the Geiger."

"All right, all units," Bahr said. "Circle at a quarter-mile radius from Number Seven. Ground units alert for encirclement. Use caution. Whatever's in that circle, keep it in there, but do not attack. Repeat, do not attack. Out."

He turned to Alexander as Carmine came stumbling up through the muck and rain. "You drive it," Bahr said. "Now get it moving."

He knows you, Alexander thought. *He knows you, and he's playing this little game out, just waiting for you to break.* There was no longer any question in Alexander's mind about his being investigated. But McEwen could get him off the hook. He'd known McEwen back in Mexico, when McEwen was training with BRINT. McEwen would help him…

Viciously, Alexander slammed the controls into full drive. The car screamed out of the soft, muddy rut, siren going.

A mile down the road they approached the helicopter cluster. Alexander hit the brake button and the Volta squealed to a rocking halt. Bahr jumped out without a word to Alexander.

The DIA ground troops were already trotting into the drenched brush and forest, their hand-flashes bobbing. Probably veterans of the crack 80lst, Alexander thought, the legendary guerilla army that had been fighting the war of containment in the East Indies. British Intelligence used the 81st to forge stubborn links in the Asian economic and political situation.

The DIA had their pick of these men, and to date there was no record of anyone resisting arrest by DIA agents.

"Strike!" the squawker boomed again. "Ground Unit Three."

Bahr's voice grated from one of the 'copters. "What do you see?"

"Nothing clearly. It's hot, though…"

"Get some flares in the air. Bring your circle in tighter, but hold fire…" Another voice came in.

"Mr. Bahr? This is Johnson, at the Plant. Three U-metal slugs are missing from Number Four pile. Dummies loaded instead."

"Good work," Bahr's voice came back. "That about clinches it. We've got them cornered out here. Sit tight."

Stunned, slack-mouthed, Alexander slumped back in his seat, his heart barely beating, cold sweat forming on his palms and forehead. A dead, crushing weight seemed locked inside his chest.

Three slugs missing.

Even McEwen could not help him now.

His Security system had let three U-metal slugs, each weighing fifteen pounds and furiously radioactive, get out of the compound. And his career…he swallowed, a bitter taste cloying up in his mouth.

Once Bahr got those three slugs, he was finished.

Somewhere in the sky a flare burst, throwing dead white light down on the treetops. Alexander pulled himself out of the car and stumbled up the hill into the woods.

Beyond the closing circle of men, Alexander could see something. It lay in a clearing in the trees, vaguely defined in the harsh flare light…something large, gray, and flat—a disc.

Somebody was shouting close by, "Looks like some kind of a flying saucer! Put a camera on it."

Quite abruptly the gray disc in the clearing rose a few feet off the ground. Yellow spikes of energy crackled beneath it. Seconds later it blossomed out like a violent orange flower. The blast wave of the explosion struck Alexander like a fist hurling him flat. A flame-colored cloud mushroomed upward, burning furiously, then sputtering out in a wave of intense heat. The 'copters still in the air closed in.

CHAPTER TWO
A Ghost from the Antarctic

NUMBLY, Alexander flexed his fingers a couple of times, feeling his wrist artery hammer revealingly against the polygraph cuff.

Bahr was saying. "All we want from you is the truth. Just a few simple facts. You were Security officer there. You admit you devised the system. Our investigation is going to turn up facts eventually…you'll help yourself if you save us some time."

"I've told you everything I know," Alexander insisted.

McEwen, sitting on one side of the room, motioned to Bahr. From the corner of his eye Alexander watched them whisper, the elderly DIA Director mumbling low and inaudible, shaking his head.

John McEwen had arrived. McEwen, the white hope, the letter-of-the-law defender of National Stability and the Vanner-Elling way of life. He'd taken one look at the gaping crater five miles north of Wildwood, and ordered a complete news blackout, isolation of the area, and scrambling of all communications. This action was almost without precedent since the bleak days of 1995-96 when the panic wave that followed the Crash was at its bloodiest.

Bahr had outlined the observed facts to McEwen, and McEwen had accepted the most obvious explanation. The three U-metal slugs missing from the Plant had been carried by person or persons unknown past the road alarm and loaded into a vehicle in the woods, which blew up when searchers approached it.

When Alexander had protested and brought up such details as the questions of method, motive, and the silent exit monitors at the Plant gates, Bahr had countered angrily with charges of obstruction, interference, non-cooperation and concealment. He tore into the tardy arrival of Alexander's Security troops.

Finally Alexander had played his trump…the blatant illegality of Bahr's DIA unit forcing an inventory at the Plant. McEwen muttered something unintelligible about Project Frisco, and walked back to stare into the crater again. Alexander had been packed into a 'copter and flown to Chicago for questioning.

The questioning had started six hours earlier.

So far neither Alexander nor Bahr had given the slightest indication of their previous acquaintance, imposing their own private rules in this cat-and-mouse game of polygraphy in which Alexander was the carefully calibrated mouse. But the questioning was getting sharper. Bahr didn't tire; already Alexander could feel fatigue catching up with him.

It was only a matter of time before his ability to pick his way through the razor-edged questions would begin to falter and confusion and bewilderment would set in.

And he knew this was more than just a routine interrogation.

Bahr was undoubtedly remembering Antarctica…

Vividly the memory of it flooded back to Alexander. Bahr had been in the Army then…a sergeant in *Communications Command*, assigned to the tiny post in the early warning net that stretched across the frozen Antarctic continent.

Alexander's mind placed the date instantly: July 12th, 2019. Just three days after the first radar alert, when the scopes of Station 1743, buried deep in the Antarctic ice, had picked up three unidentified objects moving at precise orbital speed over the lower end of South America at an altitude of 800 miles. It was an altitude three times higher than anything flown since the satellites had been scuttled and the infamous Moon rocket project had been abandoned back in the 70's. An immediate report had gone to the special intelligence section of DEPEX, and the entire Western Bloc went into Condition B...preparation for H-missile attack.

Antarctic Station 1743, Alexander's command, was the chief early-warning unit between Southeast Asia and the vital South American population centers. It was expected that the first hostile move from the Eastern Bloc would be an armored H-missile plunging into the buried station from a 600-mile altitude. The station had been living on coffee and hyper-stimulated fear for forty hours, the air reeking with sweat and adrenaline, the men snarling at each other with increasing tension, when the sergeant had come into Alexander's office.

"I want six hundred sedation units," he said.

"What for, Sergeant?"

"I am going to put half the personnel under sedation for twelve hours," the sergeant said, "before we have a riot."

"That's impossible," Alexander said. "We're on Condition B."

"If we're hit, it won't matter whether we're sleeping in bed or souped up on a Benny. But if those men out there stay awake any longer they'll tear each other apart."

Alexander had known that the tension was growing but he was in command of the station, and a Condition B could not be ignored. "Suppose you let me make the decisions about the welfare of the men, Sergeant," he said sharply. "That is not your responsibility."

"You stupid idiot," the sergeant said distinctly, "if I didn't make it my responsibility you'd have been cashiered out of the Army in a week for snaf! Do I get those sedation units?"

"No!" Alexander managed to choke out. "Get out of here. Get back to your station."

Sergeant Julian Bahr turned on his heel. The heavy plastic door slammed, and he was gone. Four hours later, in the mess hall, one of the men began beating on the table with a heavy plastic cup. Someone began to scream. In a moment twelve hundred men were screaming, cursing, yelling, the benzedrine-stimulated fear and frustrated helplessness erupting in volcanic pandemonium.

At the decibel peak of this first crescendo, Alexander walked into the mess hall, unarmed and alone. He knew he might not live but the riot had to be stopped. What he said was drowned in noise; and he was facing a closing circle of hate-filled faces. With coffee mugs and table knives in their hands they crowded toward him...

Something seized him from behind. Someone jerked him out the door, half-carried and half-dragged him down the corridor, up a flight of stairs and down another corridor to the weapons room. Groggily he saw Bahr kick the door open. Then with a heave Bahr threw him through the inner door that led to the weapons rack.

Heavy-duty stunners lined the racks, carefully secured by a steel bar and padlock. "The key, give me the key," Bahr demanded.

"You're not going to touch those weapons," Alexander told him bluntly. "I'm still in charge of this station."

Bahr didn't answer. He slammed the inner door and bolted it as the sounds of the pursuing mob grew louder in the corridor. As the first pounding of cups, feet, fists and shoulders began on the plastic door, Bahr crouched in front of the weapons rack, his hands gripping the six-foot-long steel lock bar. He began wrenching at the bar, his huge back and legs straining.

Alexander pulled a low-powered stunner out of his pocket. "Get away from that rack," he said. "Those men will take my orders or face mutiny charges. I'm not going to have anybody doing any killing or paralyzing."

"Drop dead," Bahr sneered.

Alexander fired. Bahr screamed and hit the floor. The stunner should have paralyzed his whole body in a rigid knot, but it didn't. Somehow, unbelievably, he grabbed the back of a chair and hoisted himself erect, his right arm, neck and side frozen in the position he was hit, his right leg jerking in agonizing spasms. Bahr swung the chair, hitting Alexander across the face. The stunner flew out of his hand across the room.

Contemptuous of the odds against him, Bahr faced destruction.

Dazed, Alexander saw the big man drag himself across the room, using the chair as a crutch, his right leg and arm flapping. Alexander watched incredulously as Bahr seized the padlock in his left hand and slowly twisted the lock apart, the hard steel snapping with a sudden crack. Bahr tore the lock-bar off and pulled a sleek heavy-duty stunner from the rack as the plastic door cracked under the savage pounding, spilling a dozen men into the room.

What happened after that Alexander learned later in bits and snatches while he was recovering in the Buenos Aires Military Hospital from a fractured skull and a broken nose. Bahr, armed only with an unloaded stunner, drove the rioters back into the mess hall, and though half-paralyzed, marched six hundred of them through twelve-hour sedation shots, ordering the four frightened lieutenants around like puppy dogs.

With half the station sedated, he sat at the head of the mess hall, stunner across his knee until his leg stopped jerking and his right side functioned again.

Condition B was called off long before Alexander came out of his coma. No H-missile attack had occurred, the unidentified objects never reappeared in the sky.

Alexander received a letter of commendation for his excellent handling of the riot, and Julian Bahr was court-martialed out of the Army for striking an officer.

The court-martial was already over when Alexander regained consciousness. Bahr had refused counsel during the proceedings, and sat silent throughout the trial, glaring at the Board of Officers with such open hatred and contempt that only consideration of the extreme circumstances saved him from Leavenworth.

Once out of the hospital, Alexander had tried to reopen the case, but there was little official interest. Nothing Alexander could do, they had informed him, could influence the observed facts recorded on Bahr's permanent Stability Record: that the man was contemptuous of authority and prone to violence, a dangerously unstable personality, and hence a serious Stability risk. Under the basic principles of the Vanner-Elling government this meant that Bahr would never be allowed to climb above a green-card position in any career he might choose.

But now, across the room from him, behind the glaring lights, was the same Julian Bahr, unquestionably a top lieutenant in DIA, the most powerful and mysterious of all governmental agencies...

"Now," Bahr said, stepping around in front of him. "We've given you every chance to help us."

"I've told you everything I know," Alexander protested. His heart began pounding as he saw one of Bahr's men move a small sterile tray within his range of vision. The tray held two syringes, and an alcohol sponge.

"You're lying," Bahr said. "We know that. We've considered the possibility that you may not be lying deliberately."

"I'm not lying," said Alexander.

"What security system was in force when you took command at Wildwood?"

"Standard Army, Class Six."

"Why wasn't that system still in effect last night?"

"Because I ordered it changed."

"What plan did you substitute?"

"A modified Bronstock plan."

"You devised it?"

"Yes."

"Why did you change the security system?"

"I felt the old system was not good enough. Class Six is next to no security at all."

"And your plan was better, I suppose?"

"Yes."

Bahr leaned down to him savagely. "Tell the truth, Major. Was it blackmail? Or were you bribed?"

"You're out of your mind," Alexander said.

"Didn't you tell me last night that no U-metal was missing?"

"Yes."

"Was the U-metal missing?"

"Yes."

"Doesn't that prove that your security system had loopholes?"

Alexander groped for a way out of the trap. His eyes were burning from the glare of the lamps; his mind wasn't functioning properly.

"Well?" Bahr said.

"There were no loopholes."

"What was your post before Wildwood, Major?"

"Bureau of Information, New York."

"Your position?"

"Director."

"Why aren't you still there?"

Alexander's hands clenched the chair arms. "It's on the record, you can look it up."

"I don't have time to look it up. Why were you downgraded?"

"There was a routine stability check," Alexander said hoarsely. "I was re-evaluated, and reassigned."

A cold smile crossed Bahr's face. "Your position in BURINF was an important one, wasn't it?"

"Yes."

"It gave you considerable national prominence, considerable power..."

"Yes."

"And then they dumped you in a sludge-pot like Wildwood."

"They couldn't do anything else," Alexander protested. "I was getting shaky. The psych-men had no choice but to reassign me."

"Who bribed you, Major? What was the loophole in your security system at Wildwood?"

"There wasn't any loophole."

Bahr threw up his hands. "We're getting nowhere. You admit your security system broke down. There must have been loopholes. You won't tell us what they were. We'll just have to stimulate your memory." He pulled the syringe tray toward him.

"You can't use that," Alexander protested. "I have not been charged with any major crime or espionage. I have no legal counsel here. And only qualified therapists in DEPCO can use drugs, after a case has been properly reviewed."

"He's right," McEwen said wearily from the side of the room. "He's on sound legal ground."

Bahr turned to the older man.

"This is an emergency. The man is obviously lying."

"We can't help that."

"Mac, Project Frisco itself may hang on the information he has..."

"The law is the law, Julian," McEwen said, "Project Frisco or no Project Frisco. You can't deep-probe this man."

Bahr's eyes glittered. For a moment his heavy, impassive face started to twist with rage. Then he shrugged.

"All right. We'll hold him and try to clear it through Washington. Let's check the teletype now and see if anything new has turned up."

When Bahr was gone they took off the pressure bandages, the perplates and salivators, the respirator and the restraining jacket. "Cigarette, Major?"

He nodded, inhaled gratefully. Like many people of ability and imagination, Harvey Alexander feared more than anything else the psychologically abhorrent process of having his brain picked by strangers. Now, having escaped it, he was almost dizzy with elation hardly noticing the skilful hands that were attending him, until he felt an itching in his nose, and went to scratch it.

His wrists were bound.

He strained and thrashed, and found his ankles strapped too. A huge light was being lowered from the ceiling. Above him, like serious, pale, eager-faced gargoyles, were Bahr's young men.

There was a sudden sharp pain in his thigh.

He screamed.

CHAPTER THREE
The Leak

IT WAS the break Julian Bahr had needed since the very beginning eleven months before, and now when there was something for him to grab hold of, John McEwen had decided to put on the brakes.

McEwen was saying. "Julian, we're out of our depth. We're dealing with something we can't handle by ourselves..." His voice quivered and he spread his hands helplessly.

Bahr choked down his anger and impatience. In the early days of his DIA work he had liked McEwen thoroughly, and felt a powerful obligation to this fatherly, impeccably honest older man who had salvaged him from the drunken, thwarted existence he had sunk into after his court-martial from the Army.

But McEwen had changed. Since the beginning of Project Frisco, Bahr had watched him crumbling, bit by bit, until it seemed incredible that this sick-looking creature could be the same man that he had known before.

Something out of the ordinary had been going on. Nothing tangible...a dozen incidents nobody could explain, patterned only in that they did not fit any reasonable pattern of normal occurrence. The theft of a commercial codebook reported from a San Francisco office. Scattered unexplained radar pickups fanning across the Midwest over six month's time, without identification of target. The hijacking of a thermite truck on the New York-Chicago Expressway, followed a week later by six simultaneous thermite fires over a hundred-mile area, photographed by chance by a passing jetliner. The disappearance, under highly questionable circumstances, of several dozen men in key scientific and government posts...

The presence of any imponderable in the delicate social and economic machinery of the country under the Vanner-Elling eco-government was intolerable. The balance of power between the Federation Americas in the west and the Sino-Eastern Bloc was far too delicate to permit unexplained incidents. That balance had teetered once, in 1965, and the world still bore the scars of that brief, bitter war. After the violent economic crash that had engulfed the world in 1995, a different sort of balance had been forged, but still a balance.

Project Frisco, under Julian Bahr's diligent direction, had thrown the entire striking power of the DIA into a swift, silent search for a pattern behind the occurrences.

For eleven months they had run up against a blank wall…a thousand leads traced down, leading nowhere. No clue to the enemy's intentions, nor even to the enemy's identity. Only the growing conviction that the pattern was hastily conceived.

And now, for the first time, a chink in the armor, a possible break…

And John McEwen was afraid to go on.

"Listen to me, Mac," Bahr said. "We've got something here at last that we can get our hands on!"

Weakly, McEwen shook his head. "The DIA has its limits, Julian. An atomic theft…this is out of our hands."

Bahr's face hardened. "Mac, we can't back out now even if we wanted to. We've got to hang on if it kills us."

"I…I don't see…"

"Whoever stole that U-metal made a mistake. A very bad mistake."

"Mistake?" said McEwen.

"There was nothing wrong with those exit monitors. They were working fine. You couldn't get a radium-painted watch dial past them without tripping the alarm, and they were permanently sealed so they couldn't have been disconnected."

McEwen looked up. "Then you think Alexander was telling the truth?"

"Not necessarily. But some things have checked out. Whoever took that U-metal out of the Plant had it so effectively shielded that it didn't trigger the exit monitors."

McEwen blinked. "But that doesn't make sense. The very minimum shielding for that stuff would be a foot-thick slab of lead. Nobody could have carried that out past the guards."

"A man could get a property pass," Bahr said softly.

"For a truck load of U-metal and shielding?"

"Oh, no. But maybe for a briefcase."

"You're not making sense," McEwen said. "Those slugs…"

Bahr slammed his fist down on the desk. "Mac, *it happened.* Of course it doesn't make sense, there's no earthly way anyone could cram those slugs and shielding into a small package and waltz out the gate with them, but that is exactly what must have happened." His eyes were bright on the Director's face. "All right, suppose a special shield was used…a very special shield, say, maybe just a monomolecular layer of neutrons packed in tight, like the tiles in a mosaic…an invisible skin built into the wall of a briefcase, completely impermeable to any radiation…"

"There isn't any such shield," McEwen said flatly. "If the Eastern Bloc were within five years of something like that, British Intelligence would have told us long ago. And nobody in this country is working in nuclear physics…they don't even dare talk about things like that any more for fear DEPCO will be down their throats…"

"In other words," Bahr said quietly, "there is nothing known that could be used as a shield like that."

"What do you mean?" McEwen said hoarsely after a long moment. "What are you trying to say?"

"I'm saying that we've been trying so hard to pin all these occurrences down to the Eastern Bloc, that we've ignored what was staring us in the face," Bahr said. "Nothing has fit together, but these things have been purposeful, just the same. Those thermite fires…all six burned in front of searchlight reflectors and beamed *straight up.* The high-frequency signals we've been trying to pin down…not messages, not traffic or Morse characters, just *signals*…"

Bahr stood up, his huge body filling the room. "What have we been looking for, Mac? A Chinese guerilla unit? A Ruski intelligence team? Maybe even a BRINT unit checking our reaction speed? We've been looking for something we could recognize and classify, something we know…and we haven't found it. But *nothing* that we know could have gotten those slugs out of the Wildwood Plant."

McEwen's face was gray. "Julian, if there were a remote possibility…"

"I saw that explosion last night, Mac. I saw the thing before it exploded. That U-metal would be worthless to any human agent, but to an Alien intelligence team, it might be a different story. We can't guess what they might have wanted it for. Their idea of intelligence might be as different from ours as…as DIA from BRINT."

Slowly, almost feebly, McEwen fumbled in his pocket, pulled out a white box and took out a capsule. "What do you think we should do, Julian?"

"First, sew up last night's incident tight. That means blackout of all news stories, and indoctrination of the areas where the power failed. Make up a cover story to give them, and make it good. BURINF can take care of that…"

With an obvious effort of will John McEwen straightened up. "If there's a leak…if even a hint gets into circulation…it could be worse than the crash."

"There won't be a leak," Bahr said confidently. "We'll keep everything to do with this incident and any new ones under top security…but most important of all, don't use the word Aliens in any communications. Don't hint at it, don't joke about it, don't say it, or write it, or think it. Because if there *are* Aliens…"

With all the force and precision of a guillotine blade, the blackout fell on the incident of the Wildwood Power Plant raid.

The cover-up was fast, and skillful. From somewhere in BURINF there emerged a newscast story of a power line failure between Wildwood and St. Louis, causing a power blackout the

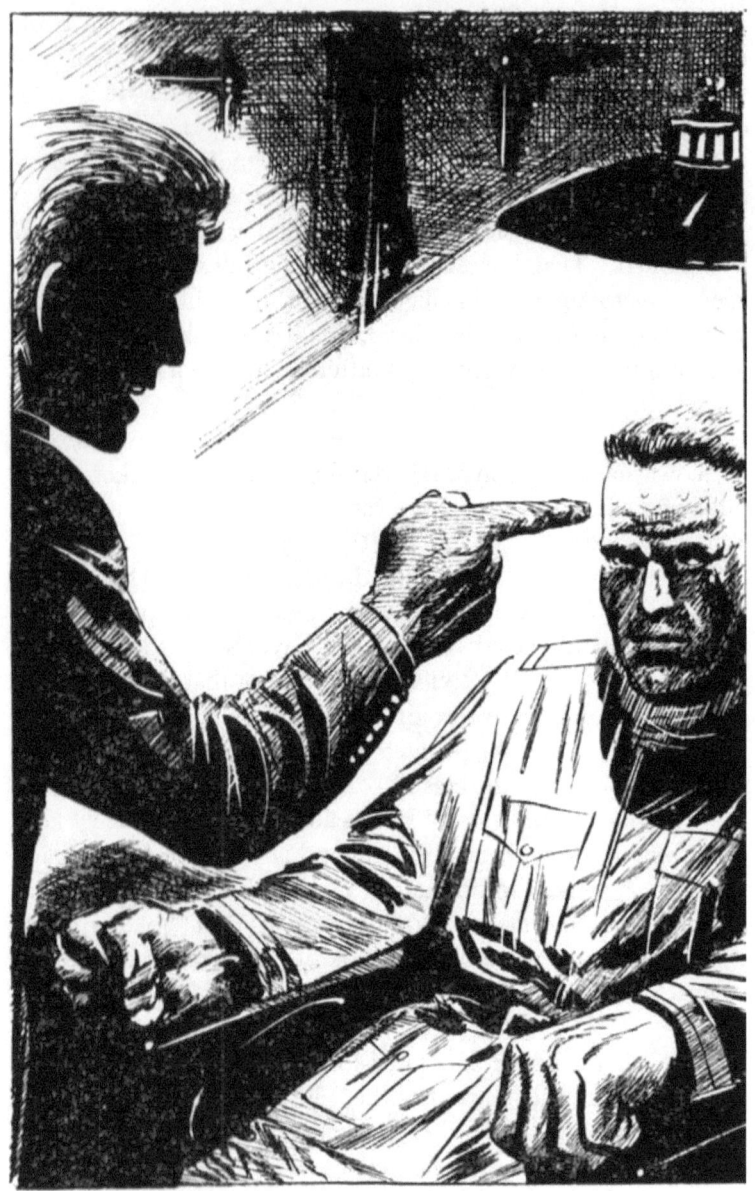

He had no answers to the vicious questions.

previous night. Broadcast over a tightly controlled net to reach only St. Louis and its suburban centers, it reassured everyone and explained everything, even though it was a complete and deliberate lie.

North of Wildwood *Road Washed Out* signs went up on all wheel-strips leading within twenty miles of the crater. Major Harvey Alexander's absence was covered, and the cordon of young, serious-faced DIA men circulating in the Plant area was explained as a team of auditors evaluating the Plant operations to prevent another breakdown.

It was done swiftly and efficiently, but to no avail.

When the leak came, it was from a totally accidental and unforeseeable source.

Station WDOM-TV in Jefferson City, Illinois, reported that a local hunter in the bush had been awakened by an explosion in the region of the Wildwood Power Plant. A forest ranger had also seen the blast, and noticed the concentration of helicopters in the area...

Bahr only caught the last few lines before the commercial, but that was enough. Cursing, he ordered the story squelched, and the phone line to WDOM began buzzing.

But the move was not fast enough; already Station BCQN in Canada, on a network that was not under DIA censorship, had called WDOM for details. Someone at the station blundered and said the story was being killed. Fifteen minutes later, in a scheduled newscast the Canadian station opened the dike.

"A mysterious explosion in the vicinity of the Wildwood, Illinois, Atomic Power Project, has become the subject of a furious DIA censorship move," the announcer said. "Earlier this evening Station WDOM-TV reported two eye-witness accounts of the strange blast, which occurred shortly after midnight, but further details have been totally suppressed. In spite of the censorship move, however, an amateur radio group TBX-57HC3 picked up some police frequency radio chatter last night, originating in the blast area. TBX has provided us with a tape recording of this chatter, which we have edited somewhat in preparation for this rebroadcast..."

Bahr was on the phone personally before the first sentence of the newscast was finished. He listened to make sure it was going to be as bad as it sounded. Finally he was connected with the manager of the BCQN station.

"This is Julian Bahr, Assistant Director DIA, speaking for the Director. We've just caught the beginning of your broadcast, and you seem to have some misinformation about the situation here at Wildwood."

"Really?" The manager's voice was languid.

"We'll be glad to give you a complete picture of the situation in another half hour, but we'd like to request that you hold off on that broadcast. It might cause confusion to have different interpretations of the event in circulation."

"Yes, I should think it would," the manager said.

"Then you'll cancel the broadcast?"

"Oh, I'm really afraid that would be out of the question, Mr. Bahr..." The voice was regretful, but quite firm.

Bahr caught the remark from the radio about the tape recording, and realized instantly that TBX was a cover code for one of the Canadian intercepts for British Intelligence. He covered the mouthpiece with his hand.

"BRINT picked up our 'copter chatter last night," he said, looking at McEwen's white face.

"They've got to kill it," McEwen said hoarsely.

Bahr uncovered the mouthpiece. "We would appreciate it very much if you could hold that broadcast, somehow," he said, throwing up the lure. There was no time to lose.

"Er...do you think we could get a reporting team into the area?" That meant, of course, a BRINT intelligence team.

"I doubt it," Bahr countered, curious to see just how eager BRINT was. "We'll give you a complete report..."

"I'm not sure that would be completely satisfactory. We really can't wait that long and then there's the matter of how much you *can* tell us."

They *were* eager. Very eager.

"Well, but the Wildwood Plant is a highly classified government project," Bahr said. "Not that *I* doubt your discretion."

"Of course, I understand the problem you have with Security," the manager said, warming to the bargain. In the background Bahr could hear the first fragments of 'copter-chatter coming through...his own voice, directing the Unit Seven 'copters toward the strike area. "Still, we *do* have an obligation to our public to verify newscasts as thoroughly as we can..." Meaning that BRINT knew something was in the wind but hadn't pinned it down yet. Bahr cupped his hand over the mouthpiece and turned to McEwen and Carmine.

"BRINT wants in. Badly. They must have flushed Project Frisco and..."

He never finished the sentence. Quite suddenly McEwen clutched at his chest and moaned, his eyes bulging. His breath went ragged, his face turning blue.

"Get a doctor," Bahr roared, slamming the phone down. "For cripes sake get a doctor!"

A doctor arrived in a few minutes, but it was too late. McEwen was dead. The diagnosis: coronary occlusion precipitated by overwork and sudden shock.

As the white-coated ambulance attendant carried the stretcher out, Frank Carmine put a hand on Bahr's shoulder. "Well, Julian," he said, "it looks like it's up to you, now."

CHAPTER FOUR
Bahr Wins a Skirmish

LIBBY ALLISON, makeup pencil in hand, was trying ineffectually to smooth her dark red hair and paint her mouth back into shape as the small private elevator shot up from the lobby of the New York DEPEX building to DIA headquarters on the eightieth floor.

Julian should have called her when he got back into town the previous evening...but of course he didn't. Instead, there was a visit from Adams that morning in her office at DEPCO. Little weasel-faced Adams, with his warm professional smile and his cold eyes watching her. Libby shuddered. Everything in her years of psychologist's training screamed out whenever Adams came near her...

Not that Adams had mentioned Julian, of course. No request to review her casework on him, no suggestion that a machine-analysis of her reports on him might be in order...nothing as straightforward as that from the DEPCO Director. Just a lot of smooth jargon about the threat of an aggressive, unstable, ambitious personality to the smooth functioning of a Truly Stable Society and "thoughts" on her sworn duties as a Department of Control psychotherapist to help identify and weed out such unstable personalities before they could constitute a threat.

Adams hadn't said a single word about Julian, but it was there; he had been talking about Julian every inch of the way, and he knew that she knew it.

And after Adams had gone, Libby knew for certain that something had happened last night, something bad, and that Adams knew about it, and hence DEPCO, and that neither. Adams nor DEPCO liked it...

The elevator stopped, and Libby stepped across to the DIA reception desk. The girl put through her call when she saw Libby's white DEPCO card.

Bahr answered. She listened to his invective. A moment later she put the phone down and smiled warmly at the receptionist. "He'll see me," she said.

The long, high-ceilinged DIA headquarters was the center of a storm of subdued but feverish activity. Everywhere was a flurry of clerks, division heads, scribes, all so feverishly intent on what they were doing that they nearly tripped over her as she came down the corridor.

The door to McEwen's office was wide open. Julian Bahr sat at the Director's desk, the cone of a dictating machine in one hand. Frank Carmine was nearby.

Libby came forward, refusing to accept Bahr's evasion.

Here was the center of the sense of urgency and tension that pervaded the place. Bahr's face was tense and angry, his eyes bloodshot, his mouth a hard, confident line. With her trained psychologist's eye Libby could see the danger signals like foot-tall handwriting on the wall. The controls, the adjustments she had tried so hard to build into his personality were beginning to snap, one by one...

"Julian, I want to talk to you." He slammed the microphone down and pulled her to the side of the room. "Damn it, Libby, I can't see you now. Go on down below and I'll be down when I can break away."

"We have an appointment now."

His scowl deepened. "I told you I'm busy."

"I know you're busy. So am I. That's why I've got to talk to you now."

"Look," he said, "I've got a Condition C problem to handle, and a new job to get under control. I don't have time for your...interview."

"All right," she said, "then I'll drop your case right now. I'll have another worker assigned to you tomorrow, if you like. A man, in case you don't want any more...interviews...with women."

Bahr stared at her, his face heavy with anger. She knew she had struck his Achilles heel...his savage, almost pathological fear of the DEPCO mind invaders, the one beast in his twenty-first century jungle he did not know how to cope with. He glared at her, his hand still clenching her arm. Then he nodded to the anteroom that still had his name on the door, and, pushed her roughly inside. He kicked the door shut and turned on her. "All right, what do you want?"

"Julian, what's going on here? Where's Mac?"

Bahr told her. It was like a slap in the face. "We're keeping it out of the newscasts until we have things under better control. Of course we notified the key government people."

"But...*dead.*" She shook her head helplessly. Now there was no doubt why Adams had come to her office.

"So you're the Director now," Libby said.

"For the time being, yes. I can't let this Project sag while DEPCO bickers about a new appointment."

"Oh, it won't sag! Not with Julian Bahr running things." She turned on him viciously. "You should have seen yourself out there! The Commanding General, whipping his whole Army into trembling readiness. You love it, don't you? Blood pressure up, adrenals pumping, ego swelling up like a purple balloon..."

"That's about enough from you!"

"Not quite enough, Julian. Adams was in to see me this morning. You're going to have to resign as Director."

"Resign! But I've been working for five years for this job."

"I know that. I've been watching you, and I knew all along it was coming to this. You can't keep the job. DEPCO won't let you."

"They've got to let me," Bahr said flatly. "Nobody else knows what Project Frisco is...not even BRINT. They're going out of their minds over there; they don't even know the cover-name for the Project. But since last night, Project Frisco is a Condition C operation. We aren't dealing with Eastern Bloc activity, Lib. It's more than that."

Then he told her about the U-metal, and the exit monitors, and the whole story.

"You mean you think something extraterrestrial was responsible for the raid?"

"For everything. Heaven knows how long it's been going on. The thermite fires, the disappearances...did you know that John Cullen vanished from his home last night? There's no man in the country who knows more about our Stability Control system, and now all of a sudden he's gone. Libby, somebody's got to track this thing down and find out what's happening while there's still time." He stopped suddenly. "You think I'm lying, don't you?"

"No, Julian, I think you're telling the absolute truth."

"You don't think I can do it, do you?"

Libby did not answer.

"And you don't want me to try," Bahr said bitterly. "You'd rather have me stick my neck in the yoke like a work horse and let somebody crack a whip over me. Well, I've taken too damned many orders, and now I'm going to give some."

"Julian, you just won't understand."

"You'd like to stop me, wouldn't you?" he said. "Push me back in the rut. Punch some new holes in my Stability Card and dump me back at the bottom of the heap again. That's what you want, isn't it?"

"It isn't what I want or don't want," Libby said wearily. "If you won't step down now, I can't protect you any more. You'll have a DEPCO man in your office before you can turn around. You'll never know what hit you. They'll find that you're unstable and dangerous for anything but a green-card job. They'll take one look at your real Stability profile, and down-grade you right into a fruit picking battalion."

Suddenly he laughed. "I don't believe you," he said. "You've been handing me this Stability garbage for five years now. Always trying to make me stop pushing...as if I couldn't handle the job. I assure you I can.

"It's not that," she said. "It's what you might *do* in the job. And I've been covering for you, believe me, but I can't do it any longer. If you don't quit this job right now, I can't help you any more."

He walked around the room, slamming his fist into his palm. "'Okay," he said unexpectedly. "I'll quit, then. But I'll need time to get Project Frisco straightened out, first."

"How much time? Two days? Three?"

"Heavens no! I couldn't get anything done that soon."

She shook her head. "No good, Julian. I've got to have a definite date. You're up for an automatic DEPCO check right now. You can't get away from it...the best I can do is stall them. And if you won't give me a definite date, I'll call them right now."

"For crying out loud, what do you want me to do?" Then he

stopped, searched her face. "Libby…"

"I mean it, Julian."

"You're bluffing," he said. "If I get my stability clearance revoked, it's your neck too. There goes your career. Think about that."

"I already have." Libby turned and picked up the phone, dialed the DEPCO exchange.

Bahr watched her make the connection all the way through to Adams' office. Then he hit her with it.

"You'd better think about Timmy before you make that call," he said.

Very slowly, Libby put the phone back on the hook and turned to face him. All the fight was gone from her suddenly. She felt weak, and sick. "You couldn't be that rotten," she said. "Not even you."

"I want this job."

"Julian, you promised."

"Things are different now. And I'm not going to do any favors for somebody who's selling me down the river."

"Julian, he's your child too. I'm entitled to one child with my job rating. I'll raise him and support him. I won't tie you down or even ask for partial support. All I want is your signature and a BHE test. Is that asking a favor?"

"You can stand a five-point cut in your Stability rating," Bahr said brutally. "I can't. I can't even stand a DEPCO review. Particularly when my therapist has been…"

"Julian! He's your son! I don't want to lose him. Do you want him to go through the same thing you did…the Playhome, and Playschool, and Techschool and everything? You don't know what those schools are like now. They didn't experiment with the children when you went…"

"Those are DEPCO projects," Bahr said. "That's your outfit running them…don't you like them?"

"There's a lot about DEPCO I don't like, that's neither here nor there…"

"Then get them changed."

"They're all right, most of the time. Most of the kids come through all right, as long as they're not too stubborn or independent. But what if he's like you, Julian? What if he fights back?"

"Then good for him. I took it, he can."

Libby pushed away from him, looked at him coldly. "I could name you anyway, and have you dumped as a Stability risk for refusing to accept paternity."

"And I can get eight men to swear you picked them up and took them to bed without a prostitute's license. Eight men who can keep up the story under polygraph."

"Julian," she said, "what makes you so rotten?"

"You're the psych doc. You ought to know." Then, inexplicably, she was in his arms, and he was crushing her against him, his face in her hair, his hands digging desperately into her shoulders. "Oh gawd, Libby, I don't want to fight you. I didn't mean it about Tim. I swear I'll quit this job just as soon as I can get things under control, but it means too much to me right now, it just means too damned much. You've got to go along on my terms…"

"I know." She tried to keep the tears back, clinging to him. "But believe me, if you start to go off the deep end, I'll turn your case over to DEPCO lock, stock and barrel."

Bahr laughed, and, tipped her chin up gently, kissed her. "That's fair enough. You watch me…"

The intercom crackled. "Julian? We've got a BRINT man on the wire here."

"What does he want?" Bahr snapped. "I can't talk to him…"

"I think you'd better," Carmine said. "There's been a landing up in Canada. BRINT won't let us into the area unless you head the team yourself. They want to know right away."

"Hell," Bahr said. "Tell them yes. I'll be in the air in three minutes." He snapped the speaker switch to off.

"Julian…"

"Not now, not now. This is important. You stall that DEPCO team," he said. "I don't care how you do it, but stall them."

Then he was gone. She walked around the room cursing him for the things he could do to her, and cursing herself because she couldn't fight him, biting her lip trying not to cry.

Two people. A man who could not possibly understand, or give a damn, and a woman who could not help loving him.

She found the elevator and started down for street level.

CHAPTER FIVE
A Ride With the Dead

HARVEY ALEXANDER accepted the proffered capsule and popped it into his mouth while the nurse and attendant watched.

The nurse nodded. "That should hold him for another eight hours," she said.

"He's on the list for recoop in the morning," the attendant said. "Doc says around nine."

Alexander leaned weakly back against the pillow. His eyes were already beginning to blink. As the nurse and attendant left, he opened his eyes and turned his head sharply, listening to hear if the door locked from the outside. The solenoid lock did not buzz, and he leaned back with a sigh. Very sloppy. He opened his mouth and lifted the not-yet-dissolved capsule from under his tongue.

During all the dizzy, kaleidoscopic period while he had been recovering from the deep-probe, escape had been evolving in his mind. There was no question that his neck depended upon his finding out what had actually happened at the Wildwood Plant. He was certain that Bahr's investigation would never clear him, even if McEwen would back him to the hilt. He would be recooped, and treated with chemo-shock, and wind up in a fruit-picking battalion with a new name, a new identity, and a blacked-out memory.

He looked out the window of his room. The hospital was surrounded by a ten-foot wall, with guards at the gates. He was undoubtedly in a maximum-security wing that could be reached only by elevator, or by passing guards. It was a suburban hospital, undoubtedly the George Kelley.

And that, he thought, was a break…

When he had been assigned to the Wildwood Plant, Alexander had spent several weeks studying all the major security systems of note in the world: prisons, psychotic wards, A-plants, computing centers, the Kingsley mines, the Chinese and Soviet political camps. He had also studied the Kelley system, modeled on the Bronstock system used in Eastern European "rehabilitation" centers. He had found no noticeable weakness in the Kelley system at the time, but then he had been on the outside, not the inside.

And that, he decided, made a very great deal of difference.

He opened the door a crack, ear pressed against the aluminum sill, listening for the telltale vibrations of the alarm gongs used in the Kelley. There was nothing. Somewhere below, he knew, a master panel lit up any time a patient's door was opened, but it was nearly dinnertime and most of the personnel would be occupied. Even the hall TV scanners were dim, though he knew the slightest alarm would instantly throw the hallways and rooms under surveillance.

He padded across to the men's lavatory and ducked inside. He collected all the toilet paper rolls and hand towels he could find and crossed swiftly back into his room.

It took only moments to crumple the paper and towels, wrap them in a sheet from the bed, and stuff them under the sponge-plastic mattress. There was a bed light on the wall; he pulled out the plug, ripped the lamp off the wire, and bent the naked copper ends into a neat pair of lobster claws.

Finally, he dropped the three metal toilet paper rollers into a pillowcase stripped from the bed. Pulling all his clothes off, he plugged the lamp cord back in the wall socket and touched the lobster claws together near the nest of torn paper. There was a shower of sparks, and the fuse blew, but he blew gently into the paper nest and was rewarded by a tiny flame.

The power came back immediately on an emergency circuit. The smoke was already beginning to pour from the heated sponge mattress. Choking, Alexander threw the door into the hall open and peered out as smoke began to billow out.

As he had expected, there was a turnoff at the end of the corridor, with a civilian guard posted. Alexander waited until the smoke in the corridor grew thick enough to haze out the nearest TV scanner. Then he screamed, "Fire!" and ran toward the guard, with the pillowcase blackjack held out of sight.

The guard jerked up in surprise, staring incredulously at the man running at him stark naked down the corridor. On the dead run, Alexander swung the pillowcase.

As soon as the guard hit the floor Alexander unzipped the front of his light-blue duty coveralls, hoisted the limp form to his shoulder and hurried back to the room. Smoke was billowing out the door, and in the distance he heard the fire gong clanging. Alexander held the coveralls and let the guard slide out of them like an egg yolk. Once into the coveralls, he shoved the guard's body into the smoke filled room.

At the end of the corridor there was a sudden burst of noise…undoubtedly the fire squad. Alexander took a deep breath and plunged into the smoke. He seized the guard's ankle and began to back out slowly, coughing noticeably as the first of the emergency crew arrived.

Eager hands helped him pull the guard, face down, out of the room. Someone started artificial respiration, and Alexander coughed into his hands and backed away as more people and equipment began to arrive. Twenty seconds later Alexander was walking slowly away, past several interns who were hurrying toward the noise, and into the main wing corridor of the George Kelley Hospital.

With the first step behind him, Alexander moved swiftly toward the service elevator. It was only a matter of time before somebody noticed that the victim in the smoke-filled room was a guard and not a patient; he had to get beyond the hospital walls before the security alarm went off.

He found the morgue in the basement, adjacent to a loading platform in the rear of the main part of the building. He reached it through an employee's stairwell and a concrete tunnel leading past the power pile.

Chicago, like all major cities, had a central autopsy room, and the Kelley, like other hospitals in the city, shipped all its cadavers there on a day-to-day basis. The transit was usually made at night to avoid traffic on Wahanakee Drive. Now Alexander saw that the two-wheeled truck was still waiting, backed up to the loading platform while the drivers were in the cafeteria for coffee. There were four stretchers, with sheets covering the bodies, loaded into the back of the refrigerated truck.

Alexander scrambled up the tailgate, and climbed in back of the stretchers.

He heard the drivers returning, and crouched down half-covering himself with a sheet. Heavy footsteps came to the back of the truck. The tailgate squeaked up. The doors closed with a clang, and he was locked with four bodies in a black, freezing coffin.

Then they were rolling...

He waited until he was certain the truck was on open throughway before he groped forward in the darkness until his hand touched the gyro mount.

The gyro was one of the air driven Robling types, very simple, very reliable, the flywheel driven by a tiny stream of air impinging on the peripheral turbine blades. Once it was in motion, very little energy was needed to keep the heavy rotor turning at a high enough speed to stabilize the truck. The flywheel and turbine blades were shielded, but directly under the pressure nozzle there was a slot to let the air out.

Alexander moved his fingertip up gingerly until he felt the turbine blades nick the tip of his fingernail like a buzz saw. Then he pulled one of the toilet paper rollers and rammed it up against the spinning turbine.

There was a shower of hot sparks. The turbine screamed. The whole truck bucked and toppled with a long skidding crash, wrenching the doors open and hurling the four corpses out on top of him on the ground.

There were curses from the cab as the drivers piled out. They shoved the corpses…and Alexander…unceremoniously out of the way, and crawled into the truck with the flashlight, peering at the gyro.

Alexander slid into the shadow of the truck and ran to the shoulder of the road. He slithered down into a drainage ditch as headlights approached.

There were apartment buildings nearby, and now people were running down the road toward the wrecked truck. In the distance he heard the first faint rising whine of a siren.

He climbed up and crossed the highway as the steady trickle of people grew into a crowd and jammed the traffic.

He was out…

He found an apartment building with the door wide open, the tenants out on the highway sharing in the excitement. He picked up the lobby phone, dialed a suburban Chicago number. Three long rings, and then a woman's voice said, "Hello?"

"BJ?"

"Yes. Who is this?"

"Harvey."

There was a moment's silence, then a cool, deliberate answer. "Oh…"

"Listen to me, BJ. This is very important. I'm over on Wahanakee Drive, at the Kingston Apartments. Can you pick me up at the parking lot by the north entrance?"

"Can't you take a cab over?" The voice was distant, noncommittal.

"No, I can't. I'm in trouble."

"I'll be right over…"

Alexander moved through the shadows toward the lot. He knew Chicago fairly well, having spent three of his Christmas vacations here during his West Point days, courting his now ex-wife, Betty Jean Wright. From her apartment to this part of Wahanakee Drive was about twenty minutes. He hoped the police would start searching the buildings before throwing up roadblocks. The Kelley would certainly notify them...and the DIA...about him as soon as they heard of the wrecked truck...and he didn't want to get BJ in trouble with the police and DIA, smashed-up marriage or no...

The crash, dirty, stinking, bloody crash that knocked the whole world face first into the dirt, knocked their marriage around, too. He saw BJ twice in the first three years, and then she told him she was divorcing him. BJ married again as soon as the divorce papers came through.

When Alexander saw her some eight years later, on his way through Chicago to Mexico, he learned that the second marriage had folded too. Of course any marriage lasting over five years in those days was a minor miracle, but BJ was bitter and disappointed about it. They got drunk together for old time's sake, but she was all walled off by then, and there was nothing between them any more...

At least six sirens came screaming up Wahanakee Drive before he heard the crunch of gravel at the parking lot entrance.

He waited until the Volta was almost past him, inching along on its single wheel; then he tossed a handful of gravel against the plastic side.

"Harvey?" The Volta stopped. He climbed in.

"What's this about your being in trouble?"

"I'll tell you later. Do you know how to get out of here without running into any police roadblocks?"

"Are all those cars after you?"

"I think *so*."

"But why? What's it all about? What have you done?"

"I just broke out of the George Kelley Hospital, for one thing."

"Out of the *Kelley*? But that's..." She looked at the blue coveralls. "Okay," she said. "Hold on."

Alexander sat silently, watching her drive as she rolled through the Kingston development; across the sidewalk, through a playground and finally onto a golf course. They came off that onto an old fashioned road, obviously built in the days of four-wheeled cars, and BJ stepped the Volta up to ninety. A moment later they merged into traffic on one of the new speedways, where the Volta could cruise along at 200 with the rest of the traffic.

BJ set the car on automatic, letting the photosight follow the white lane strip, and turned to face him.

"Now what's all this about? What did they have you in the Kelley for?"

"Recoop."

"*You?* For recoop? Gawd, Harvey."

He told her about the Geiger alert at Wildwood. She let him talk. All the bitterness burst out...

"Then you think there's something rotten in the DIA?" She asked him finally.

"What does it sound like to you?" Alexander said. "Bahr has some of the men so loyal to him that they take his orders regardless of McEwen or the law. I've got to contact McEwen, some way, and let him know. Maybe he won't listen to me, but Julian Bahr is dangerous."

"You're a little late. McEwen died early this morning. Heart attack."

Alexander swallowed hard. "Then Bahr is running the DIA..."

"Pending appointment of a new Director, yes."

He swore. "Then my only chance is to find out what actually happened to the U-metal that was taken out of the piles."

BJ frowned. "But they know what happened. DIA denies it, of course, but the European and African news nets have been jabbering about it all day. Radio Budapest has been beaming it over here in English."

"Beaming *what* over in English?"

BJ reached out and switched on the radio. She flicked the dial and picked up the nasal voice of the intercontinental *Radio Budapest* announcer.

"...still have not retracted the belligerent and idiotic denial of the theft of a large quantity of atomic materials from the atomic Power Plant at Wildwood, Illinois, by alleged interplanetary Aliens," the voice was saying. *"Radio International* has been trying to reach Julian Bahr, new head of the DIA secret police, to find out why the facts about the Aliens are not being brought into the open, but Director Bahr cannot be reached.

"Reliable sources in New York now believe that another Alien landing has occurred in northern British Columbia near the Yukon border. BRINT and DIA investigating units are now en route to the site of the landing. We will continue to broadcast the facts on this incident, in spite of the militaristic security procedures resorted to by the DIA secret police..."

BJ turned it off. Alexander stared dazedly at the radio. "I saw that thing in the woods before it blew up," he said finally. "I thought I was sick, seeing things. But Aliens—" He shook his head. "BJ, I've just been through eighteen hours of interrogation on how the U-metal got out of the plant, and I tell you it *couldn't have*. Even Aliens couldn't have gotten U-metal out of that Plant unless they used the fourth dimension to do it, and then they certainly wouldn't have set off a Geiger on the road."

"They think they know how it was done," BJ said, and told him what *Radio Budapest* had reported about a neutronic shield.

"But why? And how is *Radio Budapest* getting all this information if the Security lid is on? There must be a hell of a leak somewhere in the DIA."

"I don't know...but BURINF is nearly going wild. Even John-John got flustered on his TV cast tonight. And an awful lot of people are listening to the *Radio Budapest* reports..."

The car whizzed through the thinning residential areas. Alexander sat silent for a long time.

He realized now that he had been blocking from his mind what he had seen in the woods north of Wildwood, because he had seen it and yet could not understand what he had seen. Now he was forced to face it. He needed a plan, some simple stratagem he could act on and carry out to clear himself.

He laughed suddenly, as though some tough, unbreakable fiber in him had come to life again. "A hell of a thing," he said. "I've been in the Army for so long I've almost forgotten how to fight. They're going to have to find me before they can drag me in, and I think that's going to take some doing."

"What are you going to do?" BJ asked.

"I'm going to find out what happened to that Uranium. It's the only hope I've got, with Bahr running the DIA. If I get any information, I'll get in touch with BRINT. I can trust them. Can you drive me down to Wildwood?"

"Harvey, if these reports are true, it'll be crawling with DIA men..."

"I'll have to chance that."

"All right. We can stop at my place and get you some clothes."

"I could stand a drink, too." On the surface he felt a lot easier, but deep in his mind the questions were still nagging him.

DIA was corrupt, and Bahr, in the face of the rigid DEPCO control system, was making a power grab. That much he could understand.

But an Alien invasion...what did that mean?

CHAPTER SIX
The Tiger Snarls

Bahr Director DIA stop reference project Frisco stop John Cullen and Arnold Beck reported missing Sunday PM from Univ Mich found wandering in dazed condition Central Los Angeles by Police 2200 hours stop total forty-three others missing similar conditions stop believe important stop please advise

Bahr grinned at Carmine.

"Some of our missing people are turning up." He paused.

"I'm going to see what they've done to Cullen and Beck…"

The radioman looked up from the headset. "Another urgent, Chief. Personal from Abrams in Chicago."

The message was just three words long, and Bahr swore when he saw it.

"What is it?" Carmine asked.

"Alexander," Bahr said hoarsely. "Our nice, innocent, bumbling Major Alexander. He's broken out of the Kelley."

Carmine blinked at him. "Chief, if he gets through to DEP-CO…"

"He won't." Bahr scribbled a quick message with Project Frisco priority and handed it to the radioman. "Abrams knows his stuff. Or he'd better."

"Come on Frank. We've got to get to Chicago."

Bahr climbed into the 'copter ahead of Carmine and sat brooding and silent while the rotor whined up to speed and lifted off the ground.

"You can't question these poor devils now," Dr. Petri said. "They're exhausted."

"We can't wait," Bahr said. "I'll want each of them in a separate room, and I'll want somebody with me who can keep them awake. Is that clear?"

As he waited, Bahr thought of the return trip from Canada. A DIA car had met him at the landing field, whisked him through the downtown Chicago streets with siren at full blast, but even in that brief ride he had seen the change that had been taking place since the Wildwood raid.

There was no early-morning bustle of people on the streets. Instead, people were gathered on street corners, moving listlessly into the buildings. A huge crowd had gathered to watch the morning newscast, projected on the eight-story screen on the Tribune building, with John-John relaying the latest news from BURINF. A dozen times on the way to the hospital he had heard police sirens wailing.

He looked up as Dr. Petri came to the door, nodded to him. "All right, Mr. Bahr. But I warn you…"

One of Bahr's aides stopped them in the corridor. "There's a Mr. Whiting from DEPCO here to see you, Chief."

Bahr scowled. "Too busy," he said.

"He has an AA priority. And he says it's about this Alien business…"

"What office of DEPCO?" Bahr said, stopping suddenly.

"Foreign affairs. It's about those broadcasts."

Bahr relaxed. It was not Adams' office. He was not eager to talk to anybody in DEPCO right now, but an AA priority was hard to sidestep. "Ask him to wait, I'll be up as soon as I can."

He turned into a small white room. The polygraph operator was ready and a sterile tray rested on the desk. "All right," Bahr said to the doctor. "Bring Cullen in."

John Cullen was a gray-haired man of about sixty with a wrinkled, haggard look, stooped and squinting as if the glaring white walls hurt his eyes. He was leaning heavily on his two escorts, obviously on the verge of nervous collapse. His eyes had the raw, unnatural brightness of amphetamine-induced wakefulness.

Bahr motioned him to the PG seat. "I think you'd better have a little stimulation."

"Please…"

"Just a little adrenaline and amphetamine. You'll feel like a new man." The technician clamped Cullen's arm down, deliberately missing the vein twice. In a minute Cullen's heart was thumping desperately against the chest constrictor, his eyes blinking rapidly. "We have another dose ready, in case you begin to doze off," Bahr said.

Cullen was really quite cooperative after that. There were aggravating holes in his story, but the pattern was clear enough.

He had been abducted from his home in Ann Arbor sometime Sunday night. He could not remember how, nor what his captors had looked like. There was a long ride somewhere in some sort of vehicle, a strange room, and blindingly bright lights…

And the questions…

"Who was questioning you?"

"I couldn't see. Just a voice. An odd voice."

"A human voice?"

"No. Definitely not...not what I heard." The old man hesitated. "It didn't make sense, but I was sure it was a tik-talker."

Bahr's eyebrows went up. The tik-talker reduced speech to a burst of seven pulse characters, reassembling and unscrambling them at the receiving end. It was quite reliable, but the speech itself always had the tonal curiosities of electronically sliced language, and was easily identified by anyone who had ever heard it before.

"What were the questions like?" Here Cullen was very clear. He had been asked hundreds of questions about his work at Michigan, especially with regard to the Vanner-Elling equations and their current application to controlling the psychological and economic stability of the country since the economic collapse of the Crash in 1995.

He had refused to answer questions on one very highly classified project, and had been given repeated low-voltage electroshocks until he passed out. He could not remember being reawakened. His next recollection was wandering in confusion through the downtown Los Angeles streets until the police picked him up for vagrancy.

He also refused to tell Bahr what the project was, or anything about it, even though Bahr threatened him with more amphetamine. Cullen knew about Security, and nothing short of a BRINT unrestricted examination would have gotten topsec information out of him. Bahr made a note on the spot to give Cullen a type 4 background check as soon as things quieted down; Bahr did not like people to refuse him anything.

The following six men, far more cooperative, had also been picked up, as far as they knew, from their homes on Sunday night by unidentifiable captors. There were two sociologists, a biologist, two linguists, and one of the few physicists in the country still working on physics. They had all been questioned intensively about their respective fields, never seeing their questioners and all confirming the curious singsong of a tik-talker intermediary.

Bahr slammed the folders shut and went down to the room where the repatriates had been herded after their interrogation.

"All right, we're through questioning you for now," he told them. "When Dr. Petri is satisfied that you're in good medical shape, you'll be released." He watched the sagging heads, heard the tiny sigh of relief around the room. "However, you will be kept under full Security surveillance."

"But you've already questioned us," Cullen said feebly.

"Obviously you must realize that under the circumstances we can't assume that anything you've told us is true," Bahr said.

"But surely the Polygraph records..."

"May mean nothing at all."

Cullen was sitting up now, his face red with anger. "Mr. Bahr, we have certain legal rights..."

"As of now, Dr. Cullen, you have no legal rights. We have reason to believe that your abductors were Alien creatures who are engaged in the first steps of an invasion. From the manner in which you were abducted, it appears that the Aliens are able to penetrate our cities without detection, either in disguise as humans, or by using and controlling humans. If they have techniques of mind control that we don't know about, you men may be dangerous pawns."

He paused for it to sink in. "Now, if you have that straight, we'll get on. You will be responsible to me for everything you do or say. You will answer no questions and make no statements. If I find a single quote, admission, in any of the TV casts, I personally will be in charge of improving your understanding of Security."

Dr. Petri lead them away. Bahr pushed back his chair and went upstairs to where the committee from DEPCO was waiting.

DEPCO was a love organization. Everything they did had

love overtones. Inevitably, it clouded their judgment. Equally inevitably, it entrenched them with incredible firmness in the position of power they had held since Mark Vanner had set up his equation-control on a government-wide basis after the Crash. It was exceedingly difficult to attack love as an institution and get very far with the attack.

Julian Bahr instinctively preferred hate and fear to love, but now he knew that he had to have wholehearted, unquestioning cooperation from DEPCO. Therefore, he had to love them. While his elevator rose the six stories to the conference room where the DEPCO committee had been waiting for him, Bahr tried to think of one single reason to love the organization that was doing everything within its power to wreck his life.

He couldn't find a reason.

Love was necessary at times, of course, sometimes even pleasant, refreshing, comforting. Sometimes he thought he really did love Libby, and suffered violent pangs of guilt at the way he always seemed impelled to fight her, to try to dominate her, and wished he didn't have to depend on her faking his Stability Rating, because if she had just been a good-looking girl maybe he could talk to her frankly the way he once had talked to certain prostitutes before the custom of installing tape recorders in hotel rooms and houses.

But Libby was still a therapist who worked for DEPCO, and there were some things you couldn't tell your analyst even when she was sleeping with you.

He found the DEPCO committee waiting patiently. The leader of the group was a tall, blond haired man with pale blue eyes.

Bahr shook his hand and smiled back, through his teeth, and then he saw Paul MacKenzie of BRINT sitting at the side of the room, taking everything in. Bahr felt his shoulders and neck tighten. So MacKenzie hadn't gone to New York after all. Spying on him...

"All right," Bahr said. "Sorry to hold you up, but I had some important work in progress. Now let's have it."

The leader of the delegation cleared his throat. "I'm Whiting, Mr. Bahr. We're really sorry to cut into your time like this, but we're alarmed."

"About what?"

The DEPCO man seemed embarrassed. "About the way the DIA is handling the investigation of these...incidents that have been occurring."

"You mean the Alien ships that have been landing?" Bahr said.

Whiting winced. "Mr. Bahr, there is a fast-growing panic spreading in the country, centered in rumors of Alien landings. This morning there were closely averted riots in Los Angeles and St. Louis. Our sources indicate that foreign news listening is up by a factor of ten in the past week. Our social control techniques were devised to handle panic-emergencies, but nothing of this magnitude has ever happened before, not even during the late Crash years. If this were to explode into a full scale panic..."

Bahr scowled. "Why are you coming to me, Mr. Whiting?"

"The leaks, Mr. Bahr, the Security leaks. The foreign news nets are getting information, and the people are listening to them. Your cover stories from BURINF are simply not selling. And the foreign network implication that you are trying desperately to cover up is just fanning the flame."

Bahr shrugged impatiently. "We had one really bad break, the 'copter chatter intercepted by the Canadians." He glared at MacKenzie and said, "There haven't been any leaks since then."

Whiting frowned. "But there have! Six hours ago *Radio Budapest* was broadcasting a detailed description of an Alien landing in northern British Columbia."

"What did you say?"

"He states the news is out," MacKenzie said from the side of the room. "It's all over the country."

Bahr swore viciously. "Then there's a leak somewhere between DIA and BRINT. We've kept it so tight that—" He broke off, turned to an aide. "Tell them to get ready for a complete news blackout on all frequencies. Tell them to get those foreign nets jammed. Every news story that goes out from now on will have to clear with me personally."

Whiting of DEPCO sat staring, his face going white. "Mr. Bahr, you can't do that! A news blackout now would be the last straw!"

Bahr swung on him. "You idiot, don't you recognize a war when you're staring one in the face? Whatever this Alien is, we know practically nothing about him, and he knows everything about us. We can't even guess what his next move might be. He may have been monitoring our TV casts and newscasts for years. He's interrogated our key personnel. Everything he has done has been perfectly geared to touch off a generalized fear reaction."

"But the people—"

"The people will believe the truth. That's what we'll give them."

Whiting said, "The one thing we simply cannot face is an Alien invasion. It will tear our society out by the roots."

"Why?" Bahr said harshly.

"Because we have absolutely no defense against an Alien invasion—*none whatever*—and the people know it."

"Nonsense. We have weapons, we have technology."

"They won't do us any good against an Alien invader," the DEPCO man said. "Not in the face of fear."

"You mean the fear of space?"

"I mean the *fear of spaceships*," Whiting said. "You have no idea how deeply it penetrates. You have no idea how we've struggled to sublimate it since the Crash—" Whiting sighed, his eyes taking on a dreamy look. "Vanner recognized it, long before the Crash. He even recognized what had to be done to anchor the Vanner-Elling system, to drive technology from the minds of the masses, especially the future masses. That was the only hope for stability; and we needed stability at any price. A brilliant vision. Vanner was afraid of it, because of the repercussions, but Larchmont—"

Suddenly, Bahr tagged him. Whiting...of course! The one Libby had told him about. Whiting, the last of the pure Eros men left in DEPCO, a protege of the legendary Larchmont who had almost succeeded in converting the educational system of the country into a vast group-analysis instrument during the shaky, formative days of the Vanner-Elling government. Larchmont had not quite succeeded in putting that through, but he had left the imprint of his own occult personality permanently in the psychology of the country, and in the government.

Bahr became impatient with Whiting.

"What you mean to say, is that because of the Crash the people now have an enormous guilt-fear of spaceships, and by association, are afraid of Aliens. Is that right?"

Whiting seemed stunned by Bahr's succinct summation of the problem. "Well—yes."

"All right. Now listen carefully. We'll have to give them the truth as we see it. We can use sibling rivalry toward the Aliens, because of their humanoid form. Of course, we'll have to declassify that." He spoke swiftly, powerfully, hoping that he wouldn't get Libby's little bedroom lectures on theoretical psychodynamics so badly scrambled that even Whiting in his ecstatic state would choke on them. "Then we'll play up the non-phallic shape of the Alien spaceships, and feature protection and security as coming from a computer-guided defense against the Aliens; from the caverns, of course."

He was afraid for a moment that MacKenzie might laugh out loud and spoil the whole thing, but the BRINT man managed to suppress the reaction in a fit of coughing. Whiting was nodding eagerly.

"Brilliant!" he exclaimed.

"Certainly that approach will cut any panic off at the root," Bahr said gravely. "With DEPCO authority—from you—we'll handle the security by compartmentalizing the country, by ethnic areas; play up the we-group against the Aliens. Of course, we will need a Condition B censorship on all newscasts and travel."

Whiting looked doubtful. "That's quite a lot to ask for."

"Don't worry," Bahr said. "I'll see that the Joint Chiefs go along, if you'll back me."

"And of course there'll have to be careful work on the news releases from BURINF," Whiting said, warming to the idea.

"For a news break like this," Bahr said, "we won't want a written release. We'll need a personal address. And I'll do the talking myself…"

The broadcast was made at seven o'clock in the evening from the BURINF studios in New York, where Bahr had flown when he finally broke free of Whiting. Since noon, when the Condition B news blackout had fallen, the powerful BURINF TV net had moved into action, coordinating trailer broadcasts, reaching every radio, public address microphone and television set in the nation.

The blackout was complete, but with a single item of information coming through from all sources…that the Director of DIA would discuss rumors of an Alien invasion of Earth.

"You've got to be careful," Libby told him, checking his TV makeup carefully. "DEPCO will be watching every gesture, every mannerism. Adams was furious when he got Whiting's report. They're watching you, and I can't stall them much longer."

"Of course you can," Bahr said. "You're doing fine."

"When did you sleep last?"

"I don't need any sleep. I feel great." He nodded to a technician who signaled from the control window, got up, and walked into the BURINF broadcasting room.

The cameras picked him up as he came through the door, and he could feel the hush of voices in the darkened room…across the nation, waiting, watching him. His mouth tightened in a flat smile he couldn't control. This was the moment he had been building for. *The past doesn't matter any more, he told himself savagely as he crossed the room. Nothing matters any more except this thing now. It doesn't matter that they gave you a green card to keep you down, to break you. It doesn't matter that they court-martialed you out of the Army. All your life they've been trying to break you, trying to jam you down into the mold, and all your life you've fought back, and now you're going to win...*

He saw himself in the monitor screen as he walked to the microphone in the center of the booth, carrying his coat, his shoulder holster with the gleaming and deadly Markheim stunner showing, flanked by Frank Carmine on his right. Vaguely he heard the commentator chattering the introduction in a hushed voice.

"...Julian Bahr, Acting Director DIA, who is going to make a statement to the people of Federation America about the urgent national crisis that has arisen. Now, friends, the Director DIA, Mr. Bahr."

Bahr saw Adams, the DEPCO chief, tense and grim, watching him, and far to one side, the face of an elderly man with an unruly shock of white hair.

Then his voice came, heavily resonant, powerful, commanding and yet reassuring. "Friends, there is no longer any question that we are facing a national crisis. We know that Alien ships have made a landing on Earth, in the first wave of a silent invasion. They are among us now..."

CHAPTER SEVEN
The Man in the Middle

CARL ENGLEHARDT, lean-faced and impatient, climbed into the waiting Volta with a nod to the DIA driver. He ran a hand through his white hair, and settled back with a cigarette from his engraved titanium case as the car started up the long ramp to the elevated streets of rebuilt Washington.

He had heard of the urgently called meeting of the Joint Department Chiefs an hour ago through official channels, indicating that his presence at the meeting would be desirable, not to say imperative, with full endorsed approval of DEPCO and all the other agencies involved. Now, he relaxed for a moment, chuckling. Damn, how they hated to call him in! The fact that he was called at all only underlined their desperation. The very fact of Carl Englehardt's existence, utterly unassailable and unanswerable to any agency of the government, was repugnant to DEPCO, who in eight years of continuous study and examination had still been unable to mount a convincing case of monopolism or tax evasion against him. And it was a simple and inescapable fact that his independent existence was a major factor in the successful function of the Vanner-Elling eco-government, which had evolved during and after the Crash.

Carl Englehardt was an enigmatic anachronism. Nobody knew, for certain, the true extent of the industrial constellation he headed. The analysts and doom-harbingers in DEPCO clucked and squawked in protest, propounding theories and citing figures that Englehardt and a stable eco-government were mutually exclusive…but they inevitably had to ask Englehardt what his plans were for the next two or three-year period when they were setting up the parameters for the annual VE economic prognosis. And they had to admit, however grudgingly, that Englehardt's vast interlocking holdings were invariably the buffer that absorbed the stresses and strains of the annual VE plan.

Since the earliest days of the VE system, Englehardt had managed a balance of opposing forces with a finesse that was exceeded only by the legendary skill with which BRINT effected the balance of power in the Eastern turmoil.

Now, faced with a crisis, they were turning to him again. He knew what they wanted, and he knew, on the other hand, what he was prepared to provide. The meeting would be a violent one. But violence was no stranger to him.

Mark Vanner had predicted, almost to the week, when the society of the late 1990's—like a Hegelian pot of water absorbing energy without any recognizable change—would suddenly begin to boil. In the case of the old United States economy, it was crumble rather than boil, but the pattern of collapse had followed exactly and disastrously the steps that Vanner had outlined as much as ten years before.

The brilliant sampling and determinants theory for constructing a total sociological-economic-psychological picture of a nation at any given moment in time had been the work of the obscure British economist Peter Elling, but the mathematical extension of the theory into a workable, reliable technique for predicting and controlling the future was the creation of sociologist-mathematician Mark Vanner. He had tried in vain to convince the shaky, frightened Hartman administration that the wild, exhaustive race with the Eastern Bloc to mount permanent, manned and armed satellite ships in space and manned garrisons on the moon was leading the country to the brink of economic disaster; that unless it were stopped in time, it would inevitably lead to a total collapse of the economy. It had been clear since the early 1960's that a dangerous proportion of the national reserve of money and man-hours was being poured into defense tactics, but the continuing drain of the XAR spaceship project was multiplying with each succeeding year.

Carl Englehardt had been fifty then, chairman of the board of Robling Titanium, and in a small way a strikingly successful man. Robling had been supplying structural titanium to the spaceship project in New Mexico, the project Vanner had denounced so clearly as the economic blight of the century, and he realized that when the abreaction came, the spaceships and everything connected with them would be trampled under.

He also realized that the Eastern Bloc would wait, poised and ready, until the American economy had broken at the wheel, and then launch the all-out H-missile attack that would finally and decisively destroy the North American continent as a political and military threat.

What Englehardt did then was still considered by some to be the most colossal act of high treason in the history of mankind; by others, a stroke of military and diplomatic genius. It was during the first barely evident economic dehydration of the early weeks of the Crash that he made his proposal to the President. By having parts made in European factories, and by having the parts assembled and tested by Ferranti, and launched from British installations in Australia, Englehardt was in a position to supply intercontinental ballistic missiles accurate within one mile of ground zero with a maximum range of eight thousand miles. Such missiles had already been built and tested by Robling subsidiaries, and could be delivered to specified launching sites at the rate of ten per day. If prepared and stationed quickly enough, they could forestall the H-missile attack from the East, which was almost a day-to-day certainty.

The missiles would be delivered to the American government in exchange for food...since very soon money would no longer buy work...but there was a single condition. The Robling missiles were not for sale. They were for rent.

There would be no blueprints. The missiles would be manufactured, sealed, and aimed for launching by Robling employees. The design of the guiding mechanism and the propellant would remain the exclusive private domain of Robling Titanium.

Already the economy was splitting at the seams, the stock market lurching, strikes spreading, food supplies in urban areas becoming scarce, but the government would not agree to Englehardt's terms. There were threats, accusations, appeals to patriotism, but Englehardt had remained adamant. He did not want his designs and his technicians commandeered, his contracts and legal protection invalidated and himself impoverished and cast out by any sudden governmental confiscation of private properties during the impending crisis. He had deep-rooted, almost archaic convictions against socialization and government ownership after the still memorable experiences of the sixties.

He would not yield. Quite abruptly, he vanished. Before the government could reconsider, the complete horror of a great national economy in its death agonies was sweeping the Western

146

Bahr's voice went around the world, changing him
from a man to a symbol.

Hemisphere. In three short days the stock market collapsed and ceased to exist as an instrument of business when the New York Stock Exchange was raided and burned by panic-stricken mobs. The military struggled helplessly to contain the spreading violence, in the face of its own mounting toll of insubordination and desertions. Within weeks the value of the dollar had dwindled to nothing; in the overcrowded cities thieving, black-marketing, and even prostitution ran rampant. The embattled government withdrew to the armored sub-basements of the Pentagon to await the inevitable attack of H-missiles from the East.

But the attack from the East never came.

Gradually, the reason why became clear. Ten missiles a day were emerging from the Robling foreign interlock, paid for by the British, and guarded by the British, who had fewer scruples about dealing with private munitions makers than the American government had had. A series of highly publicized demonstrations had been conducted, proving conclusively that the Robling missiles would do all that Englehardt had promised they would do, and the British published an ultimatum that pulled the teeth of the Eastern Bloc: any H-missile launched, from either the East or the West, would be intercepted and answered by Robling missiles. The British, for the first time in eighty years of tightrope walking between the cold war powers, now held the whip hand.

There would be no H-war.

But the rising terror of the Crash continued unabated. True to the pattern predicted by Vanner, control measures snapped one by one in the face of the savage tide. Food rotted in midwestern railroad yards, while mobs roamed the streets of the huge urban centers of the East, starving and vicious. Besieging rioters broke through Pentagon defenses. In mid-August of 1997 the mobs sacked and burned the XAR atomic spaceship project in New Mexico, smashing into the compound in trucks and killing, injuring and torturing the scientists and technicians there.

Englehardt himself remained in hiding, guarded by British Intelligence forces, until Mark Vanner had organized his provisional government in New York and begun to weld together a pattern of order around a nationwide application of the VE equations. Then Englehardt reappeared. For two decades he had continued to pour his immense wealth and resources back into the Americas, in a vast system of interlocking holding companies, reopening factories during the reconstruction period and building up the network of small industries that made him the phenomenon and power that he was.

No one seemed to know what Carl Englehardt was really after...not power, nor money, nor even glory. Because he was not directly or formally in any government function, the DEPCO analysts could not get at him to poke through his mind and background to find out what made him tick.

And still, in critical times, they needed him. Now the DIA Volta let him off at the official entrance to the DEPEX building.

But they would not like the proposal he had to make.

"Our problem," said Timmins, Director of the Department of Population, "is one of defense measures. That's why we asked you to come here today, Mr. Englehardt; to bring you up to date on what information we have on the Alien threat, and to get your views on certain problems that Mr. Bahr has brought to a head."

Englehardt nodded, looking at the men in the room. Adams of DEPCO was there, cold-faced and angry. Bahr drummed his fingers impatiently on the tabletop. There was a General of the Army that Englehardt had met casually. Half a dozen other bureaus were represented. Englehardt looked back at Timmins' blond, boyish face. "I would think," he said, "that your defense measures would depend heavily on the nature of the enemy you were fighting."

"That's what I've been trying to tell them," Bahr exploded. "We simply don't have enough information. We have no hint—

not even a suggestion—of their plans. There is a very strong suspicion, however, that they can control the actions of certain humans, at least to a limited degree."

Englehardt frowned. "Do you have proof of that?"

"Not yet," Bahr said. "Unfortunately the man who might have given us the answer has escaped our custody. I'm referring to Major Harvey Alexander, the Security officer at Wildwood."

"That is neither here nor there, right now," Adams broke in. The DEPCO chief spoke rapidly and nervously, keeping his long narrow fingers very precisely before him on the table. "An even more acute problem is the public reaction to Mr. Bahr's television fiasco. Unless we can convince the public that everything is under control—that the Aliens cannot harm them—we may be dealing with a major panic."

"In other words," Englehardt said, "you are proposing to fight malaria by distributing citronella to the natives."

Adams frowned. "I don't think I understand you."

"You're facing an unknown enemy with short-range planning and countermeasures," Englehardt said. "Which inevitably puts you a step behind him. It seems to me that our only defense here is a powerful attack, or the ability to make one."

"But what are we going to attack? Our biggest enemy right now is not an Alien invader—it's *fear*. We have to deal with that before we can even think of defense or attack."

"Then harness it," Englehardt said. "Forget about trying to control or sublimate it—use it! That's what Vanner did. He put fear and panic to work for him. He made the people rebuild and start a new society."

Adams sighed. "I don't think you understand the basis of this fear reaction. Unfortunately, this is not an attack from the Eastern Bloc. This is an attack from space. A completely unknown threat."

"I don't care what it is," Englehardt said. If you launch a good overall program, something concrete and solid, your public reaction problem will take care of itself."

"A program like that would upset the stability of the nation in a week," Adams said. "We can't take that risk. We in DEPCO have made the public, Mr. Englehardt. We have been fighting to maintain controlled stability because stability is the only safe, sensible, logical way to keep our economy and sociology balanced. Vanner and his ideas were necessary, of course, in their time. He changed the direction of society. Now it is our function to keep it running in that same direction."

"Have you ever heard of the Wywy bird, Mr. Adams?" Englehardt asked. He was referring to the ancient and vulgar joke about the bird that flew in ever-decreasing spirals until it flew up its own derriere. Bahr and a couple of the military men laughed. Adams blinked and reddened. "I really can't see," he began hotly.

"I think we're getting into personalities," Timmins said quickly from across the room. "You say we have no plan of attack ready, Mr. Englehardt. If you think we should not try to keep the Vanner-Elling system in normal operation and devote our efforts to keeping the public in a good state of mental health, then what should we do?"

"Prepare a counter-offensive," Englehardt said. "Assuming that the Alien maneuvers so far have been preliminary junkets, we can expect them to mount larger maneuvers in the future. But for that they will have to have supply routes. Now, where would they stockpile their supplies?"

There was an uneasy stir in the room. Adams was suddenly sitting upright, very alert. Timmins cleared his throat nervously. "Mr. Englehardt."

"Somewhere off the planet," Bahr answered the question. "Probably in orbit."

Adams turned sharply to Englehardt. "Just what are you proposing? That we develop a radar system to pick up some sort of—of space warehouse? Some missile artillery that could intercept them when they try to land personnel or supplies?"

Englehardt said, "All the defensive maneuvers in the world won't stop them. Look, what is the biggest advantage that the Aliens have? Invulnerability. They can get to us any time they want to. Witness the Wildwood mess. *But we can't get to them because they come from space!"*

"But we can't build spaceships!" Adams exploded.

"Why can't we? We were on the verge of it in the nineties. We had all the technology and engineering we needed...it was just a matter of time."

"But Englehardt...for heaven's sake, man...*the spaceships caused the Crash.* The whole country went insane over that. You know that, you lived through it."

"The Crash came because we could not build those spaceships the way we were building them at that time," said Englehardt. "The Crash wasn't because of the spaceships, it was because of the expense, the drain on our resources."

"But it would be the same thing again. Do you want us to go through another Crash?"

"We have the Vanner-Elling system now, and the computers. We can harness them to provide a surplus in the form of spaceships the same as you have the computers set up now to provide a surplus in the form of entertainment."

"But the entertainment is necessary for social control," Adams said. "If we took away the entertainment, and counseling, and expression programs, the tensions would begin to build up all over again."

"And isn't a spaceship an expression? Just the same as a city, or a set of laws? Doesn't it represent a definite step in the development of the people?"

"A backward step," Adams said angrily. "A regression."

"Nonsense," said Englehardt.

Adams attempted to laugh. "Really, Mr. Englehardt, I think you're disturbed. Emotionally upset. It's not an unusual syndrome among formerly technical people, of course—a fixation on spaceships. Tell me, have you ever..."

"Gone to a psychiatrist?" Englehardt's face blanched. "No! Nor felt the urge, and let me tell you something else, while we're on the subject of fixation, and living in the past. Your precious DEPCO for the past fifteen years has been doing nothing but trying to stay in one place, and keep the whole country and economy in one place, and if that isn't fixation, then I'd like you to please explain just what else it is!"

Bahr said sharply, "We aren't interested in holding DEPCO up for inspection right now, nor Mr. Englehardt's psyche, for that matter. But we do have to have an aggressive plan of action. I personally can see many points in favor of being able to mount a small space fleet, if for no other reason than investigation and early warning. It's certainly a better solution than simply digging holes for ourselves, or sitting with stunners across our laps waiting for whatever the Aliens are going to do next. The question is, can we do it?"

"We have the technology," Englehardt said.

Adams was shaking his head violently. "There's no use even debating it. Psychologically it's out of the question. We're only now getting stabilized!"

"Well, I'll go along with Carl Englehardt," Bahr said, "at least to the point of letting him show us that it is technologically practical to build spaceships. I put it to a vote. To determine whether spaceships are possible and practical on engineering grounds."

Adams lurched to his feet. "This is not something to be voted on," he cried. "We can't just brush aside fifteen years' policies of social control. DEPCO has the power to approve the plans and projects formulated by the other departments, and we cannot accept spaceships as a solution. They are hostility symbols, and an economic peril."

"All right," Bahr said harshly. "You're opposing the idea without the slightest factual grounds for opposition. DEPCO hasn't investigated the spaceship problem for twenty years. You don't have a legal leg to stand on."

"The Stability Act of '05 specifically states—"

"You can recite amendments for us some other time. I'd like to see right now how many here agree with me that an investigation is a reasonable solution." He looked around, counting thumbs.

The military, of course, went along with Englehardt. DEPEX, always willing to implement new programs, went along. DEPOP, conservative and crusty as usual, opposed. DEPRE, always willing to take on another research job, and politically jealous of DEPCO's restraints on their research into DEPCO methods, went along with Bahr.

"It looks like an investigation is in order," Bahr said.

Adams jerked to his feet. "I'll stop it if I have to drop every other project in the department."

"What are you afraid of?" Bahr said. "Does a tall tower give you bad dreams? Maybe you're the one that should be seeing the analyst." The military and Englehardt were chuckling.

"I think, Mr. Bahr, that we may be over to interview you soon," Adams said acidly.

Bahr turned to Englehardt. "How soon can you give us figures?"

"Three days."

"Make it two."

"I'll stop you, Bahr," Adams grated. "I'll stop both of you."

Englehardt laughed.

CHAPTER EIGHT
Pornography as a Weapon

HARVEY ALEXANDER crouched by the roadside. He didn't know what to do. The trip to Wildwood had been a complete fiasco. BJ had dug up clothes and found an old Lieutenant's ID card for him.

It had taken two hours in BJ's Volta to reach the vicinity of the Wildwood Plant; then they ran into the roadblocks, and realized that they could never hope to get near the Plant without being apprehended. Until the heat was off a direct approach to Wildwood was hopeless; he could only hide and wait.

But for hiding he needed a city. He picked a secluded area on a back road leading toward St. Louis, and forced BJ to let him out.

With luck, she could still get back to Chicago without being stopped.

His hand touched something in his pocket, and he drew it out…money. Simple, practical, typical of BJ. She knew he had none, that he wouldn't ask for it, that he needed it. He started trudging along the road until it crossed a secondary highway strip, and he turned south. St. Louis was forty miles away.

Half an hour later headlights sprang up behind him that were too yellowed and dim to be police, so he took a chance and stepped out beside the roadstrip to thumb. The old rattletrap Hydro slowed and stopped, and Alexander climbed in, slamming the door behind him. The driver was a worker, his yellow Wildwood plant badge still exposed. He was a man, of thirty or thirty-five.

He looked Alexander over as he started the car. "In a fight?" he asked.

Alexander carefully slipped into the speech pattern of a cover identity he had once used in Mexico. "Uh? No, no me. Spill. Took 'turn t'fast. Zip. In 'a ditch." He looked at the driver. "Gimme to St. Louis, huh?"

"Yeah, sure." The driver accepted his story. He was over-heavy, with a flat moon face, and he was already talking about car wrecks.

Alexander sank back in the seat. As the car buzzed through the flat countryside, he probed at the problem against the background of the driver's chattering until a word jerked him up sharply and set his heart hammering in his throat.

Alien.

"How's that?" he asked.

"Like I said, the Aliens," the driver said. "I was tellin' my nymph last night, 'a way I figger it the second wave will be comin' in any day now, like it said in the book, and maybe there'll be riots in town, but she said maybe people wouldn't get too scared, I mean, knowin' what was comin' next, you know, 'cause they told her plenty of times in Tech School how it was not knowin' what was comin' that made all the riots so bad back in the Crash days."

"Oh."

"'Course she gets scared kinda easy that way...you know...maybe they'll wanna use her for a breeder unit or something, like they do with cows, you know, sort of like an incubator, it says in the book, and she's afraid if they do anything like that to her she won't be able to, you know, sex it up any more, she's kinda hot, y'know, and we still got four months contract to run before we switch off."

"Breeder units," Alexander said slowly.

"Yeah, the Aliens. You know. You seen the book, huh?"

"Y' got me runnin'," Alexander said. "What book?"

"The Alien Invasion book, o' course. Ain't you seen it yet?"

Alexander shook his head numbly. "Don't read much."

"You're fixated, Jack. You're really repressed. That pulpie's been goin' the rounds for six months, everybody's seen it, and with that lover-cover...say, you ain't a Book-snooper?"

Alexander relaxed slowly. "Not me. I been away." He saw now what the trouble was. Book and magazine publishing, like TV and radio, had been under BURINF control since the early Crash days, and here especially BURINF had used the double standard circulation techniques with incredible success, to carry DEPCO control propaganda to the huge urban populations. Standard publishing channels were rigidly controlled and censored. The vast quantity of "live" psych control material went out through underworld channels—porno mags, feelie-tapes, all the vile and violent entertainment and expression sops. The BURINF-created myth of the Book-snoopers provided the necessary stimulus of salaciousness and illegality to insure that the material would be widely circulated hand to hand. But a book about Alien invaders—

"You say it's been out for six months?" he said to the driver.

"Yeah, sure, you mean you really haven't read it? It was supposed to be just a story, you know, but with the Wildwood raid and the Canadian landing, and now the blackout; everybody knows it was the real thing, y'know? This is just the first wave, testing our defenses and getting hypno control over all the key people, softening us up for the big wave, just like the book says…"

"Does it tell how they're going to invade?"

"Oh, sure…right down to the button, only it doesn't say how long between the first and second waves, y'know. That's wha's got my nymph so scared. Hasn't scared me much, but that's prob'ly because I'm better adjusted. But just the same, I wouldn't want any Aliens heavin' me into a twitcher-coma, or using me for a food culture incubator, or white-mousing me, or anything…"

"Yeah," Alexander said. "You know a place I can get this book? Where are they selling it?"

"I'd let you have mine, only I let my nymph's girl friend take it to show her daddy, we kinda switch off sometimes, even if it ain't strictly legal until my contract's up, but sometimes even a well adjusted guy like me gets all tied up and can't loosten up, you know, I ain't scared at all, o'course, but some of the things that the Aliens can do can really make you shaky. You don't think that means I'm unstable, do you?"

"No, your Group-Doc has just been slipping up, not helping relax you and get you back into the swing," Alexander said comfortingly, remembering his BURINF days.

"Yeah, that's what I've been tellin' my nymph, the group-docs oughta know what to tell us about the Aliens so we know what we oughta think, it's their fault if we get kinda shaky and get screaming dreams sometimes."

The car had been wheeling through the low, drab buildings of north St. Louis. "Look, what did you say that book was called?" Alexander asked.

"Alien Invaders. You can get it anywhere."

"Well, I'll look it up. Here's where I hop off…"

The town was dead in early-morning stillness, and he headed for the downtown section. The gulf before him had suddenly narrowed, and he thought he saw the first step across.

A pulpie book called *Alien Invaders*…

It was ingenious, and deadly, and it fitted into a pattern, Alexander realized, as he sipped surro-coffee in a stall in the deserted downtown area, waiting for the city to come alive.

First, early, undetected landings, contact, perhaps psychological control of key individuals, a concentrated study of the society and psychology of the inhabitants. Then circulation of a book, fanciful enough in nature until the things it predicted began happening. Then landings that were less secretive, designed to draw attention, to feed the growing fear and panic, in preparation for the final, massive blow.

He went out into the cool gray early-morning ugliness.

Near the riverfront he found a street crowded with bars and porno mag stalls and drunks sleeping on doorsteps.

The first stand was completely out, sold out for a week. Another place the vendor started to shake his head, then blinked at Alexander suspiciously and claimed he'd never heard of the book. In a third the last copy had gone the day before. A fourth, fifth and sixth try were equally fruitless.

Back on the street, Alexander looked around him at the sluggish hesitancy with which the city was coming to life. There was none of the downtown hustle of the early job-rush. People seemed to be moving aimlessly, stopping to gaze in windows, congregating in small groups on the street corners. It was something Alexander had not seen since the early days of the Crash, when the people, not yet desperate enough for violence, had walked about stunned, realizing with painful unwillingness that the little familiar formalities of dull, dreary work were suddenly meaningless.

And now, on this morning, he saw and *felt* the same blunted apathy.

It was wrong, somehow, in the same way the Wildwood raid had been wrong, in the same way a pulp magazine called *Alien Invaders* was wrong. All not quite fitting. DEPCO, he knew, should be clocking this rumbling volcano; they should be furiously at work draining off the pressure before the explosion came. That was what DEPCO was organized to do.

But there was no evidence of DEPCO activity, and Alexander, seeing the vacuous, frightened faces passing him, felt a growing sense of alarm, as if all the twittering birds and monkeys in this nightmare psycho-structured jungle had suddenly stilled at the low cough of a stalking killer...

He found the place he was looking for with lettering on the third floor window of a decrepit plasti-brick building of the last century, GDISCO, the local warehouse of the sprawling Magazine Distributing Company. Since hardbound books were practically nonexistent except for collector's items and University archives, all books and magazines were distributed by mag wholesaling agencies, and Magdisco was the largest, and the least critical of the material it handled. Alexander crossed the street, and went up the narrow flight of stairs.

The warehouse office was empty. Alexander's eyes searched the piles of nude glossies and Playschool contraband porno mags.

"Help you?" A thin, putty-faced man with thick glasses appeared from the file room in back.

"I'm looking for a copy of *Alien Invaders*."

The man lost interest. "Sorry, we don't retail."

"I was thinking of buying in quantity. For private distribution."

"Beat it. I already got arrangements."

Obviously subtle questioning wouldn't help. Alexander's ID card was actually ten years out of date, but it looked official when he flashed it under the man's nose.

"Lieutenant Alexander, Army CI. I'm checking up on *Alien Invaders*. I want to know who wrote it, where he lives, what else he's written. And I want all the copies of the book you have."

The man looked at the card. "I—I—we don't have that information here, Lieutenant—"

"You have it," Alexander said, stepping past him to the files and yanking the first drawer open.

"Wait a minute, wait a minute—I'll look." The man fell over

himself to get to the files.

"You'd better find it if you don't want to log some poly time," Alexander said. "We might throw in a few questions about where you get the Playschool contraband over there. That's you, that's not Magdisco." Unregistered contraband, interfering with the Playschool conditioning programs, could mean recoop and very probably a new identity in a labor battalion. The man fairly tore into the files while Alexander ransacked his desk.

"There's nothing here," the man said.

"Let's have a copy of the book," Alexander said.

"They're all sold out. They've been sold out for months."

"You're lying," Alexander said. "You wouldn't be out of anything that's selling that fast." He saw the man look around wildly, ready to make a break, and he moved in fast, clamping a wristlock on him.

"I don't have any—please—I don't have any—" Alexander jerked his arm. He twisted and groaned, and then said, "Okay, okay—"

"Fast."

"I was just told not to give any to investigators. That's all. I just had orders," the man whimpered, pulling a book out from beneath a stack of glossies. The cover was a masterpiece of the art, the title fairly screaming out *Alien Invaders: How Soon?* The byline was Diff Darrel, the imprint Squid Pubs.

"Listen, you won't tell anybody I gave it to you, huh? Just say you found it here. I just get orders, that's all."

"Who gave you the orders?" Alexander said, dropping the book in his pocket. "Who was the source publisher?"

The man made a break for the door. Alexander thrust out a foot, tripped him, and fell on him hard.

He pulled the man's arm up behind him, and then noticed the small variously aged scars and realized what caused the desperate silence. Whoever was supplying him was also giving the orders.

Alexander stabbed in the dark. Drug traffic took size and

power. Only one publishing house had that kind of power, and the ruthlessness to go with it. "Was it Crane?"

The man groaned as his shoulder ligaments began to tear.

"We can find out under a poly…"

The fight went out of the man. Alexander hacked him sharply across the neck. He had his answer.

Crane…

At street level, he walked swiftly toward the corner.

When he had gone ten paces he knew he was right. All the fumbling at the files had been a stall after all, there was a two-wheeler moving slowly down the street a hundred yards behind him, with two men in it.

Still sweating from the workout, Alexander saw the car following him. He was also puzzled.

Were the stalkers DIA men? Aliens?

Who?

CHAPTER NINE
The Robling Octopus

IT WAS a dodging, running game, trying to shake a tail in a crowded city when he didn't know how many there were, nor who they were, nor what they wanted.

The only technique that could save him was to start branching trails.

He stopped in a mylebar dealer's and bought a raincoat and hat then went into a bookstore, haggled with the book dealer for a while and gave him the book back after tucking the receipt for the raincoat into the book.

Then he moved swiftly for a few blocks, detoured through a mag stand and out again when the vendor was busy, ducking quickly around a corner. He ripped open the package with the raincoat and hat, slipped the coat on, pulled the hat low, and walked off at right angles with a couple of late-lunching businessmen. He stepped into a movie house, and out a side exit, raced down the alley, slipping out of the raincoat and hat and tossing them in a trash can. He jerked his jacket off and mingled with a knot of people carrying his jacket and faking a conversation with a dumpy housewife.

By now he was certain he had shaken his followers.

The next stop was a hotel lobby. He flashed a half-credit note at a bellhop.

"Blond or brunette?"

"Information."

The boy looked him over carefully. Alexander sagged into a slouch, his mouth twitching at one side. The bellhop was satisfied. "What do you want?"

"A tape library hookup, I want somebody to file a probe for me and bring me the report. Someone with a local ID card that's up to date and cleared for financial reports."

The boy looked suspicious. "It'll cost you—"

Alexander showed him a fifty-credit note. "That should cover it." He wrote out the information he wanted.

The boy blinked at it incredulously, then shrugged. "It's your money, Jack. You can wait in the lobby."

Two hours later the bellhop was back, and as he stared at the report Alexander decided that for fifty credits it was dirt-cheap.

It was the corporation statement of the Crane Publishing Corporation. But Crane, the report said, was itself a subsidiary. Controlling interests in Crane were held by Poughkeepsie Research, owned and operated by Seaboard University, which, as everyone in BURINF knew, was part of Robling Titanium.

No one associated with the government could really be surprised to learn that any given company, however obscure, might ultimately be traced back to Carl Englehardt and his Robling interests.

Why had Crane published *Alien Invaders?* How could they have published it, without risking their multi-million-credit necks to a BURINF check and ultimate prosecution?

Alexander tore up the photo-print, and walked rapidly away.

He knew he would have to get out of St. Louis by morning. Above all, he had to get to New York, to somehow establish a contact with BRINT, not as a fugitive and possibly an Alien-influenced traitor, but as a man who had managed to keep his head and see the way through to the truth.

The report on Crane was the key, jarring the not-quite-fitting pieces down into a compact perfect fit; a quite different pattern than he had considered before, but a pattern that was unmistakably clear.

He knew now what had happened at Wildwood, and he knew he could not waste a minute. He might already be too late.

Suddenly he noticed a Hydro moving doggedly along the roadstrip below. Alexander crouched back out of stunner range, fear creeping up his spine again. His followers couldn't be DIA. They would have picked him up long ago. But if they were Aliens, why were they stalking him so patiently?

What he needed was an accomplice, so his pursuers would have another branch-point to worry about; and so he could get a truck.

It was the only way. With a truck, and a trucker's ID he could drive to New York. Plenty of New York long hauls went through at this time of night. But he needed bait, to get a trucker out of a brightly lighted diner and into an alley or motel room…

He found his prospect in the third diner he checked. He walked up behind her, grabbed her by the wrist. "Let's take a walk," he said, as he pushed her forward.

Her lips twisted into a snarl. "DEPCO?" she asked, the word sticking hatefully in her throat.

Alexander shook his head. "A friend." He tightened his grip on her wrist and started to walk her out. He paused warily at the door, then pulled her into the darkness and told her what he wanted as he slipped her a ten-credit note.

"But where?"

"There's a motel behind there."

"He might kill me…"

"He won't kill anybody, don't worry."

He watched her go back into the diner. Ten minutes later she came out with a heavyset, stupid looking man with a trucker's cap on. They walked back to the motel office, then down the darkened path toward the cabins.

Alexander moved after them, fighting down the intense wave of self-loathing that welled up in him. But there was no turning back now.

He heard them inside, heard the woman's voice, low and suggestive, then dropping into a stream of filthy underworld jargon. Then it was quiet, with only swishing sounds, and he waited for the signal. Silence. It was too quiet. He gripped the latch, turned it and burst into the darkened room.

Then he screamed as the light hit his eyes, glaring, blinding, burning white, searing his retinas.

He felt the blow at the back of his head, and the glare-whiteness dissolved into blackness...

He was in a room without windows, utterly black. He could not move his head, and he realized it was clamped into a frame on the chair. A voice was asking questions.

He had heard that voice before, years before in the Communications Command, transcribing messages from Control in Washington. He remembered now what it was. A tik-talker...

CHAPTER TEN
The Deal

LIBBY ALLISON was kneeling on the floor playing with the tow-headed baby in the playpen when Julian Bahr walked in, threw his coat on the bed-couch. He sat heavily on the edge of the relaxo, and with a half-groan, half-sigh began to pound his fist into the palm of his left hand.

Libby looked up. "Trouble?" she asked.

Bahr's only answer was a sudden vicious smack of fist against palm, as if in his mind he had just driven his knuckles into the fragile bone structure of somebody's face.

"DEPCO?"

"That too—"

She put the youngster in the playpen, and brushed her hair back. "What else?" she said.

He didn't answer for a minute or more. His jaw was knotted in anger, his huge body tense. Then he shook his head helplessly. "The nightmares."

Libby turned sharply. "Again?"

"This morning, just before I woke up." He held out his left hand for her to see. The knuckles were cut and bruised.

"Julian…"

"I was hitting the wall. I guess that was what woke me. It's the first time in two years. What does it mean, Libby? Why do they scare me like that? Why do they start coming back now?"

She sat down, holding his hand between hers. "Julian, the last time, I told you—"

"But what have I got to be scared of?" he roared. "You want to dig and poke and scrape things open in my mind, but those things are all gone now, they aren't ever going to come back again, I won't let them come back!" He collapsed into the seat, the anger fading as suddenly as it flared. "It's no good, Libby, it's just no good. I can't do it your way."

"It's the only way I can help you. And I want to help you, you know that."

"I know."

"How do you feel now?" she asked.

"Better, I guess. Pretty good. I'm hungry, though. Haven't you got something to eat?"

"I'll make some sandwiches and coffee," she said, and went out into the kitchenette.

Bahr paced up and down the room a few times, as she put the coffee on the sonic unit. Then she didn't hear him walking and glanced out.

He was crouched one knee on the floor beside the playpen, poking his huge finger at the child, who grabbed it with small uncoordinated hands. Bahr chuckled and picked up the baby and tossed him into the air. The pale blue eyes regarding Bahr with wide surprise, and each time Bahr caught him he would whisper a soft "Ahhhhhh…"

Then Bahr the lesser began to squall, and the big man glanced around the room guiltily and lowered the loud one back into the playpen.

"The kid's crying," Bahr said roughly. "Why don't you feed him?"

"I will," Libby said. She thought, *when he's alone he's different. He's a human until he thinks people are looking at him…*

She waited until he had finished his coffee before she told him about Adams' visit during the afternoon.

"You must have been out of your mind," she said. "I told you DEPCO would be watching that announcement speech. And then you stood up there and shouted to the world that we were being invaded…"

Bahr looked at her and grinned. "I put it on the line, all right. Somebody had to."

"Julian, you cut your own throat with that speech. DEPCO doesn't have to wait until they interview you. They can slap an injunction on your job on plain suspicion of instability and schedule you for interview when they have time."

"They can't do that. Not during an emergency."

"They can, and they will."

He laughed. "How many people did they dump out of their jobs during the last Condition B? Not a damned one. And they're not going to pull me out now. If they were going to do it, Adams would already have put it through after the conference yesterday."

"Did you have a run-in with Adams?"

"Englehardt did. He's the head of Robling, and he believes in doing something, instead of patting the public on the fanny and telling them everything is going to be all right."

Libby's face was suddenly white. "What does he propose to do?"

"Build spaceships and, go after them."

"Spaceships! That's ridiculous. Everyone from DEPCO right down to the Machines will stop it."

"He's got backing. The military and DEPEX are with him."

"They don't count. DEPCO has the final say on something like that."

"Well, maybe this time DEPCO won't," Bahr said sharply. "You and your damned psych-docs mumbling about symbols and fixations...the Aliens are not going to turn up for analysis. This is no little guerilla campaign this time, we may need those ships to survive. Did you ever think of that? Your therapy and adjustments aren't worth a damn when it comes to staying alive. We need more tangible things now."

"That's not the important thing right now," Libby said. "All DEPCO has ever tried to do was to change a few minor things, like wars and squalor and neurosis...and that means catching those things at the roots."

"Garbage," Bahr said. "Englehardt put his finger on it when he said we had no place to go, and that's why everybody is afraid. If they had something to do, they wouldn't be afraid any more..."

"Do you have something to do?" she asked him.

"You bet your life I have. Run the DIA. Get to the bottom of this Alien business."

"Are you afraid?"

"I'm too busy to be afraid."

"But you have nightmares."

Bahr was silent. Libby stood up to avoid his eyes. "You don't understand," she said slowly, "and you've got to understand. There are things that drive people to do things, and they don't even recognize the reason. They think up all sorts of fantastic cover stories—lies to somehow justify doing things that they just can't help doing. That's why DEPCO was set up...to spot those inner drives and dig them out by the roots. That's why I've been trying to help you for four years now, Julian, because you don't understand what's happening inside your own mind. You just keep finding reasons and excuses and urgent necessities for everything you do, and blaming other people for everything that's done to you or anything that blocks you. I've tried to show you that it's all inside you, in your own mind, but you just say no, stall DEPCO, get me a white card, I won't let them stop me..." She broke off helplessly. "You don't even know why you *want* a white card."

"I certainly do," Bahr said. "I can't get anywhere without a white card stability rating. A green card is two strikes against me everywhere I turn."

"And if you got a white card, and you got everything you wanted...then what?"

"What do you mean, then what?"

"What would you do if you had everything you wanted?"

"I'd change things," Bahr said harshly. "I'd change everything that got in my way."

"But after you'd done all that...after you'd done everything you wanted...then what would you want?"

Bahr stared at her, not comprehending. "That couldn't happen. Everybody gets in my way, tries to stop me. I could never get everything I want."

Libby sighed, and ran a hand through his hair. "On that last thing, you're right, Julian," she said. "You don't know how right you are..."

She had hoped that she had reached him somehow, that possibly some spark of contact or understanding had been struck, but when he asked her later, "Well, what about Adams?" she knew that she hadn't reached him at all. She sighed unhappily.

"I'll try to stall him as long as possible," she said. "I don't think it will do much good. Adams is suspicious, and he's taking a personal interest."

Bahr snorted. "Adams or nobody like him is going to put me out of a job on a Stability check."

"You think you can bluff him out of it?" Libby said. "Julian, there's a storm working up in my office. Aliens or no aliens, I can guarantee that you'll be up against a prelim by tomorrow…and you won't pass it."

"I passed the other probes."

"Because I told you the answers beforehand, question by question. But I can't do that on a prelim, they use a polygraph."

"They just poke around the sore spots, don't they? They skip the questions that you don't bounce on, and just dig in the soft spots?"

She hesitated. "Yes…they study the prelim awhile before they go into a deep probe."

"Fine," Bahr said. "Then you can brief me on it."

"You couldn't use dummy answers under a poly, they'd bounce all over the place. With your adrenals…"

"I can control my reactions," he said.

"Your face muscles, maybe. Not your blood pressure and your sweat glands."

"Not even under hypnosis?"

"Even then, even with suggested reactions to specific trigger questions, I still don't know if it would work. You'd have to know the questions."

"You can find out the questions."

"No," Libby said.

He stared at her. "What do you mean, no?"

"I mean up until now I could always say I'd mis-evaluated your pers scores, or I was emotionally involved and didn't know it. But deliberate faking on a prelim is a federal offense."

He sat silent for a minute. Then he spread his hands wide. "I've got too much at stake to trip on this thing now," he said. "You've got to get me past this prelim."

"I can't do it," she said. "If they caught me, I'd be through. I'd never get a professional rating again."

"I'm not talking about professional ratings," Bahr said quietly. "I'm talking about you and me."

"No," Libby said.

"I'll make a deal with you. You've always wanted to find out about those nightmares. You've always wanted to get me into deep analysis and run me straight through from scratch. You know even DEPCO can't get me into deep analysis if I block, I'd have to be willing, cooperative. All right, you get me through this prelim. As soon as I get this Alien thing and Englehardt's project squared away just enough so it doesn't take all my time...then I'll let you start analysis. I won't fight you, I'll cooperate."

"Will you take a BHE and sign the paternity papers if I do?"

Bahr nodded. "If I get past the prelim."

She leaned back against his shoulder, suddenly infinitely tired, more weary than she had ever been in her life before. "You know, it would have been so easy," she said. "All this running and fighting—it would have been so much easier if you had let me start deep analysis two years ago."

He stiffened against her. "Easier?"

"You wouldn't have the nightmares, and the sleeplessness, and you wouldn't be boiling up with hate and beating your fist against the wall in your sleep, and you wouldn't have this prelim coming up..."

"And I wouldn't have gotten anywhere." Bahr said.

CHAPTER ELEVEN
Confidential Dispatch

From BRINT USNXY to BRINT HQX LONDON
Priority IMMEDIATE ATTENTION
Distribution HQX-K7 Only

Dear Roger:

I'm using our private channel for this letter because I am quite certain that our normal channels are under constant DIA surveillance, and I cannot route my personal opinion through Julian Bahr if I hope to keep my Scottish neck in one piece and serve any useful purpose in the future.

As you might guess, Arthur and his people in the NY office are rather at a loss with the city walled off by the recent communications edict. I am relying on the usual private channels to keep in touch with my groups, and particularly with Carl Englehardt. So far every report in my hands indicates that the pot is heating at a far greater rate of speed than we had originally assumed it would.

Arthur persists in adhering to our original plans, ignoring the almost incredible pattern that has been emerging in the past weeks.

We have assumed from the start that DEPCO, with all its systematic precautions to keep emotionally unstable personalities out of key spots, would have automatically harnessed a man like Bahr very early in the game. This has not happened. His emergence confirms what I have been telling you for several years—that the DEPCO system has been in a spiraling decay since the death of Larchmont, and that something new is certain to emerge.

At this writing, that "something new" is taking the shape of Julian Bahr.

Bahr has seized the Alien crisis as his chance for power. This of course was predictable. What I could not predict was the simple fact that Bahr has run headlong into the DEPCO restraint system and broken the restraints one by one. Ironically, the DEPCO philosophy of controlling and inhibiting men like Bahr is inadvertently guaranteeing his success. If he succeeds in destroying DEPCO, there are no strong men at the top in Federation America to oppose him. If Bahr succeeds, there will be very strong central control emanating from a single point, and no chance for us to encourage internal schism as we have in Asia and the USSR.

I believe that if Bahr is allowed to reach that point, we will have lost everything we have been working for. Unfortunately, we still need him badly, and Englehardt will support Bahr at all costs in order to get the Space Project in operation. I will talk to Carl personally about this as soon as possible, but I have very little hope of dissuading him.

Meanwhile, we must be ready to cope with the political and economic changes that are about to begin. Ultimately, we must be able to either cage Bahr, or destroy him. Meanwhile, we must be alert to a purge of some kind. Bahr is very abrupt and direct in his actions. With the Alien threat to justify him, he may move without warning at any time.

I wish I could be more optimistic, but I honestly think it is all as bad as I have outlined. I think things will be tricky for quite a while, and I may have to move quickly without clearing through you or Arthur. There is one item of genuine promise, the matter of the elusive Major that I mentioned before. Here is a man who has successfully thwarted Bahr and remains at large. He can be extremely useful to us—or extremely dangerous. I am bending all efforts at present to locate him; Saunders had his trail in St. Louis, but lost it. I will have more to report on this at a later date.

Meanwhile, if you see some brilliant chess move that will put us back in a position of advantage, contact me without delay through Talbot. Repeat, night or day.

Best wishes,
PAUL MACKENZIE

CHAPTER TWELVE
The Traitor

AT ONE A.M. the phone jingled and Bahr, still sleepless, reached over and seized it.

"Abrams, Chief. I just wanted to coordinate with you on discontinuing the search."

Bahr sat upright. "On what?"

"The drag—for Alexander. I'm pulling in the field units now."

"Scrambler," Bahr said. "Four three nine. Baker." He punched the scrambler buttons on his own phone and tested. Then: "What in hell are you talking about, dropping the search? Did I give you orders to drop it?"

A long silence. "No—but—"

"You get those field units back into operation in three minutes, or I'll green card you so fast—"

"But, Chief—he's been picked up."

"Where?"

"East St. Louis. Another DIA unit. Didn't you get the report?"

"Must have been a slipup in the tracer relay," Bahr growled. "They're probably trying to locate me now." Then, cautiously, "Which unit picked up the Major?"

"They didn't sign through the roadblocks as a unit," the man said. "It was on a personal chit."

"Whose personal chit?"

"Carmine's."

"You're certain it was Alexander they picked up?"

"Positive, Chief. There's no mistake."

"Okay, drop the search. I'll pick up the story from this end. And thanks for the call."

Bahr hung up and dialed the locater relay. "Bahr speaking. Any calls for me?" He knew before he asked that there had been no call.

"No call, sir."

"Where can I locate Frank Carmine, DIA-43?"

"He's in transit now. Destination, Red Bank, New Jersey. Field Unit HQ there. Planned arrival two A.M. Shall I try to make contact when he arrives?"

"Just deliver a message. Tell him to meet me at 2:30 at the Red Bank Ground Terminal. There won't be any answer. I'll be leaving shortly for that same destination number."

He was resetting the scrambler when Libby sat up, turning up the light. "Trouble, Julian?"

"Go back to sleep," Bahr said. "I've got to take a little trip."

"But you've got the prelim tomorrow..."

"I'll be back. It's only over in Jersey."

"You can't take the prelim on no sleep. The suggestions won't cue in properly if you're too tired. We can't risk all the work we did this afternoon—"

He continued placing his call, and motioned her to silence as it came through. "Bahr speaking. Get one of the dummies ready. He's to take a 'copter to Rahway, and a ground train from there to Red Bank Ground Terminal. Tell him to get there at two-thirty. No, nothing else, just report back afterwards. And," he added, "tell him Condition B when he hits Red Bank. Use his stunner if he has to. Double A security on this, too—and see that his stride is right. I take big steps."

"Sending a dupe?" Libby asked.

Bahr nodded as he disconnected the alarm from his Markheim stunner on the knee table, hefting the sleek, surprisingly heavy weapon thoughtfully.

"What is it, Julian? Aliens?"

"Maybe," Bahr said, dressing hurriedly. "Where are the keys to your Volta?"

"On the sill. But what do you want the Volta for?"

"If anyone calls, I'm on my way to the ground terminal. Don't mention the Volta." He tucked the stunner into his shoulder holster.

"You're not going there alone! Julian—"

The door closed quietly behind him...

On the way Bahr thought about his association with Frank Carmine.

Frank had been a year ahead of Bahr at Fort Riley, and with other veterans of the 801st, had wound up in DIA after his ten-year tour. McEwen, founder and director of DIA, was looking for a man to keep his field units coordinated and working under pressure. One of the veterans of Baker Three had said wistfully, "What we really need is a man like Julie Bahr to light a fire under this outfit..."

Carmine was assigned the task of locating and approaching Bahr. Bahr knew little about DIA, but the appeal of the old camaraderie, and the opportunities for control and power rang a bell.

Bahr soon began to exert much more power under McEwen than the organizational charts credited him. As his power increased, he found people who were eager, willing, and desperate to help him. In a world of unstable personal relationships and obviously cardboard leader figures—senators, congressmen, and especially chief executives who were put in office chiefly on the basis of appeal, good looks, friendliness and the knack of projecting "sincerity" through the TVs—the segment who wanted someone powerful and confident to identify with gravitated to men like Bahr.

His followers were many, and of all the dependables, the most loyal, the most devoted, the most unswerving was Frank Carmine.

Which was why, when Bahr found treachery coming unexplained and unheralded from a source that would have seemed least suspect, he did not surround himself with other DIA subordinates who were close to him.

It was not by accident that he had not been notified of Harvey Alexander's capture. And if Carmine could defect—

Shortly after reaching Jersey, Bahr picked up two henchmen, Jule Chard and Stash Kocek.

It was two-forty, and Bahr looked out of the phone booth at Kocek, who was sprawled indifferently on one of the benches in the Red Bank Ground Terminal, and then up at the clock.

Two-forty. There had been no sign of Carmine, nor of Bahr's double who was supposed to have arrived at the terminal by monorail ten minutes before. Bahr wondered, suddenly if his whole DIA organization had been infiltrated and seduced into an anti-Bahr putsch. But the motivation—that was the puzzle. He could not credit Carmine—small, sad-faced, balding Carmine—with the drive, the personality, the political ambition or the money to mount a secession against him.

Chard appeared suddenly. "What's wrong, Chief? I thought Carm was going to show."

"Something got fouled. There should have been a mono in here ten minutes ago. Check with the station office and find out what went wrong."

Chard hurried off. He was back a moment later, almost running. "Crackup," he panted. "The mono jumped off the L-ramp just north of the station, went through a guard rail. Eighty-foot fall. They haven't even put out the fire yet."

"All right, fine," Bahr said.

"It'll take Carmine a while to get back to the DIA HQ here to smooth out an alibi. We can beat him. Carmine's got a surprise coming."

Three A.M., and from the cruising Volta Bahr saw lights on the first floor of the two-story building that housed the local DIA HQ. The building was on a corner, but there was an apartment building next to it a story higher.

Chard drove around behind the apartment so they could get in through the service entrance. Bahr checked his watch. "Wait for my signal, then get the wires," he said to Chard. He waited with Kocek until the Volta moved off into darkness. Then they started up the stairs for the apartment roof.

Two minutes later they had slid down the fire-escape poles onto the roof of the DIA building, and with Kocek's skeleton key let themselves into the roof kiosk.

Quickly Bahr and Kocek searched the upstairs rooms, found them empty. There was no sign of Alexander. They waited. Then somewhere down below a door slammed; there were noises, voices shouting something unrecognizable, then Carmine's flat nasal monotone cutting across the hubbub.

"...eighty feet off the ramp. Ten people aboard, but we couldn't have squeezed them off without alerting him. All dead, concussion, heat and suffocation." There was a note of pleased satisfaction in the flat voice. "We saw them identify Bahr, all right."

"No, no calls."

"Good. I've got to call long distance."

Bahr nudged Kocek and grinned. Then he crossed silently to the window and flashed a recognition pattern with the infrascope at the Volta parked down the street.

"Chard will cut the main power line into here," he whispered to Kocek, "I think there are seven of them...what's your count?"

"The same."

"All right. Chard will come in the front after he cuts the wires. I don't care about the rest, but I want Carmine alive. I've got a few questions for him."

Abruptly, the light downstairs went out.

"Hey!" a voice cried. "The lights—"

"Where's the fuse box—"

In the noise and confusion Bahr and Kocek darted down the stairs and crept into adjacent corners of the main room, letting their eyes focus in darkness.

There was a flicker of movement toward the door, and Bahr's stunner ripped at full lethal power, the sub-echoes ringing. A scream and a thud. Silence.

"In the corner—" Carmine's nasal voice. There was the snigger of a burp being cranked. Bahr fired again, his target perfectly picked out in the infrascope. Body and gun hit the floor at the same time.

Three down.

"Bahr?"

"Over here, Chard. They're in the cardo room. We'll have to flush them." He crawled silently, checking four bodies, guessed at three left in the cardo room. "Kocek—those concussion eggs."

Bahr unscrewed the safeties, knelt and tossed one egg inside the cardo room door. There was a dull crash, and the glass blew out of the windows. The second toss was against the rear wall. A burst of orange light flared and a man came screaming into the hall clutching his ears. Bahr cut him down with the stunner.

One left.

"Carmine!" Bahr stood up, stunner ready. There was a scrambling sound. "Don't shoot him," Bahr said. A couple of shots scattered around the room as Carmine fired wildly. "I'm coming after you." There were scurrying noises; Bahr smelled smoke, saw a flare of burning cards across the room. He saw Chard leap across to smother the flame, and cough and reel back as three slugs struck his chest. Bahr fired the stunner once, an off-target narrow beam shot and Carmine screamed.

Bahr hurled himself on the thrashing, half-paralyzed man, tore the gun out of his hand and drove a knee into Carmine's groin. There was a shrill agonized cry, then retching.

"Get that fire out." Bahr jerked Carmine up by the collar, smashed his fist into his face savagely twice, and hurled him out into the hall.

Chard was dead. Bahr shrugged, as the whole wall began to flare from the burning cards. "Get out to the car," he said to

Kocek. "I'll get Carmine."

He thought suddenly of the prisoner. Alexander...where was he? He shook his head. No time to search the rest of the building, the fire was getting worse.

But he had Carmine, and Carmine would talk. With Kocek to persuade him, Carmine would beg to talk...

"He'll break," Kocek said confidently as they moved out into traffic. "We'll find out who put him up to it."

Bahr didn't answer. Who put Carmine up to it was important...but now the interview with Adams that was looming up in two hours was more important...

In the darkened basement room, Alexander lay immobile, staring fixedly at the ceiling, and he smelled the smoke long before he felt the heat of the fire. He tried to move his arms; the muscles responded, but slowly, sluggishly, and he fell back against the couch, panting at the effort.

There was no one up there who could help him now.

He tried again to flex his muscles. It was useless. The place was a smoke-filled oven; already he could see the yellow brightness of the flames in the crack under the door. He knew the truth now, and it was possible that he knew things that nobody else knew, but he would never be able to tell anyone, to use that information. It was useless to fight any more, but he tried.

Slowly, he hitched himself up on his elbows, began inching his way across the room toward the door.

He had almost reached it when—choking on the acrid fumes from the fire down below—he saw the uselessness of it.

He had been running too long. Now there was no more chance, to run...

CHAPTER THIRTEEN
Tiger Trap

LIBBY saw Adams' feet propped up on her desk. The elevator had closed behind her. The office secretary had seen her. Adams had seen her.

She turned on her most charming smile, but all she could say was, "Good morning."

Adams did not smile back. She knew that he had made his mind up already what he was going to say and think and listen to any attempt to ignore the fact would simply debase her a little more. Her only hope now was to beat him to the punch and keep feeding him answers before he could get the questions out. And Julian was not there. Where in hell was he?

"I guess you're waiting for Mr. Bahr," she said.

"Of course I am," Adams said coldly. "Where is he?"

"He had an emergency investigation last night," she said. "He may be a little late getting here." She shifted nervously.

"If he gets here at all," Adams said.

"He would have notified me if he couldn't make it."

"I see."

Silence. Then Adams said, "I'd like to see your case history on Bahr."

"It's not quite up to date. I have some notes in my apartment."

"We can probably manage without anything from your apartment," Adams said acidly. "I want to see what you have here."

"It's up to date as of two weeks ago," she explained, sliding her safe drawer open. "Mr. Bahr has been too rushed for scheduled analysis." Even before she got the drawer all the way open, Libby sensed that something was wrong. Someone had been tampering with her files. She hesitated.

"Would you mind?" Adams was on his feet beside her, lifting the folder out of her hands. He retired to the chair, leafing through the folder, pretending to study it. Obviously he was stalling. He knew what he wanted to find; he was just hoping to draw some comment from her by the long delay. She did not oblige him.

Finally he looked up. "Are you familiar with the function of a DEPCO therapist?"

"Certainly I am."

"How would you define it?"

"Helping people."

Adams gave an impatient shrug. "All right, flood relief helps people, too. Is that what you mean?"

"Helping them to adjust their emotions and thinking processes to living in the world," Libby countered. "Helping them gain insight into—"

"Miss Allison, you've recommended Julian Bahr for six grade changes in the last four years. Do you call this adjustment? When you let a highly questionable individual accrue more responsibility and power with every upgrade? When you put more and more strain on a sick personality?"

"He's my case. I think the diagnosis is my responsibility. And the treatment."

"As long as you remain his therapist, yes, but when you become his agent—"

"I'm still his therapist," she said.

He raised his eyebrows. "Really? I thought this might have changed since his appointment as Director of DIA."

"It's only a temporary appointment."

"Temporary. Of course. And he's still under treatment? Coming along nicely, too. Am I right?"

It took strength to control herself. "You have the case history there."

Adams' glanced back over the report. "No analysis, I see, after four years. Didn't you think he needed analysis?"

"I wasn't able to convince the patient—until recently—" Adams dropped the folder on the desk with a thud, and her voice trailed off.

It all sounded so weak. Even knowing in advance what Adams was going to ask didn't improve the story. She had been deluding herself; she could see it now, coldly, unhappily. She had been used. Even the most impartial witness, reading that case history, could see that she had twisted, bent, and sidestepped every principle, regulation, safeguard and normal channel in DEPCO to do Bahr's bidding.

Therapist. She felt suddenly sick; for the first time she saw, in stark, uncolored light exactly what she had been doing.

Twelve years of training, six years of hard-earned experience, and she had thrown it all out, a life's work, to play lover to a sick, ruthless brute.

A Phi Beta Kappa concubine—

The phone was ringing. Adams picked it up. "It's Bahr, for you. See that he gets here."

Libby took the phone. She flicked on the local muffler so Adams could not hear.

"Julian? Yes, I know you're late. All night? You knew you had this interview today." Damn him, she thought, *damn* him! "I meant what I said, Julian... if you don't come over for the prelim today, Adams will have an injunction against you tomorrow morning. This is one hundred percent under DEPCO jurisdiction. Yes, you're damned right I'm looking after my own neck—if I lose my rating—that's what I said, by tomorrow morning. All right, I'll tell him, and Julian—"

The phone went dead. She hung up, trembling, and turned back to Adams.

"He'll be right over," she said.

Julian Bahr was stepping forward to the open door of the big DIA Hydro when a plush black Volta spun in to the curb. "Julian! Julian Bahr!"

Providentially, it was Carl Englehardt. "Let me drive you somewhere, Julian. You've seen my report?"

Bahr nodded, and got into the Volta as his men started the Hydro behind them. He looked at Englehardt. The man looked more tired, yet miraculously younger than he had three days before. He was smiling.

"Why all the bodyguards?" Englehardt asked. "Is that customary?"

"I was assassinated last night," Bahr said.

"You hardly look it. You got the assassin, I presume."

"No, no leads at all yet." He didn't care to advertise rot in his own backyard. "But something will turn up shortly."

"And the Aliens?"

"Nothing. A couple more missing men are back, all with the same story. Things are, just too damned quiet, I don't like it."

"You've got my report on the spaceships now, you know what I can do," Englehardt said. "If something stalls now, it could be very costly. It could end everything."

"I'm doing all I can to push it through," Bahr snapped.

"Is that enough? You know I'll back you all the way— money, technicians, influence—but it's got to move, or we're lost."

"I'm having trouble with DEPCO," Bahr said. "They want to pull me off the job until they're satisfied that I'm dull, normal and inert. By DEPCO I mean Adams."

"You never impressed me as the sort that Adams would be likely to stop," Englehardt said.

Bahr's jaw clenched savagely and his fist smashed against his palm. "Adams won't stop me," he said. "Not if I have to break his back with my bare hands. As long as I still have friends I can count on—"

Englehardt laughed. "A man as ambitious as you are, really has no friends, only victims. If I were you I wouldn't count on anybody helping for one minute after I lost complete control. In fact, if I were you, I might worry about my life, if I had no more DIA to protect it…"

It was Bahr's turn to laugh. "Killing is my game," he said, "and I always win."

"Well, I think this is where you're going," Englehardt said as the Volta slowed in front of the DEPCO building. "I will see you this afternoon, Julian?"

"You'll see me," Bahr said, and walked into the building.

Bahr was smiling when he came into the office. "Sorry I'm late," he said. "Shall we get started?"

Adams rose slowly, "This is a routine examination, Mr. Bahr. You realize that. When an individual moves into a job as important as yours, there are just a few precautions that have to be taken, for the public good."

"Fine, that's all clear," Bahr said equably.

"All we want to do is ask you a few questions, and ask you to give us frank honest answers. These questions will help us make a few simple evaluations on your personality, Mr. Bahr. I think it would be best to let the machine warm up, and let you get adjusted to it...are you familiar with the polygraph?"

"Who isn't?" Bahr sat sprawled in the surro-leather chair. He let Adams fasten the apparatus with his thin bony fingers, then waited through the usual pointless recounting of what they were going to do.

He watched Libby maneuver into a position where she could watch the polygraph and still see him to cue in his suggested reactions. Bahr could feel his palms begin to sweat a little. Why didn't she throw out the first cue? Damn she hadn't already sold him down the river—?

She rubbed her right ear, which was the first trigger, and Bahr could feel the automatic cue-word come into his mind as Adams began the questioning.

It was simple at first, so ridiculously simple that he wondered why he had feared it so long, but then the questions began to blur and he grew tired, felt the weariness creeping up, and the boredom. It was the boredom that worried him. He'd made three complete runs so far, and obviously Adams wasn't getting what he wanted because he was already talking about still another repeat. Libby was looking too pleased for things to be going too badly, even though Adams was scratching far afield of the normal questions looking for reactions to snap onto.

Then the hooker came.

"I've done my best," Adams said, shaking his head, "and I guess there just isn't any sense to making another run after three confirmations—" He began to loosen the pressure belts, and Bahr gradually tensed, knowing something was coming.

"I'm sorry, Mr. Bahr," Adams said sadly. "I really am, and I'd do anything I could to avoid having to do this. But in a job like yours, we can't have people who are dangerously unstable—dangerous to us, and dangerous to themselves." He smiled unhappily. "Sometimes in emergency situations some people just naturally shift into an authoritarian mold. Sometimes pressure forces people into adopting a personality structure that is—well, dangerous to the society and themselves. They should be grateful, we should all be grateful that we can detect this sort of thing in time to…"

"Hold it," Bahr said, jerking out of the seat and grabbing Adams by the shoulder, his big fingers digging into the man's frail body. "You're not railroading me," he roared. "You couldn't do the job I'm doing, or even get into a job like it, you're not going to…"

"Julian!" The stark urgency in her voice stopped him for an instant, and Libby tried to say something to Adams, but Bahr was angry now. The post-trance suggestions were overridden by this new threat, and his whole body seemed to swell with rage. He shoved Libby roughly aside and seized Adams with both hands, lifting him off the floor. "You queer! You lousy, pasty-faced queer, I'll flatten your face out on your own polygraph if you try to…"

"Julian, *stop it!*"

He dropped Adams. Libby motioned him to bend over so she could whisper in his ear. "He did that deliberately to trigger you. Your PG was negative; three times, he had nothing on you until you grabbed him and started to open your mouth…oh, Julian, why did you have to lose your temper?"

Bahr stood silent, shaken, cursing himself for not immediately realizing what was happening. He had promised to take his cues from her, but the minute there was a real threat—

he just couldn't depend on anybody else.

And now Adams had what he wanted—violence. Ego identification with power and job. All the things Libby had warned him about, all spilled out in one stupid burst of rage.

This time there would be recoop and a labor battalion, sedation, his daily ration to supplement a fuzzy prefrontal, and all the other permanent, irreversible precautions to make him safe, stable, and happy.

Adams got up slowly, shaken, white-faced, but glowing with triumph. "All right," he said in that saccharine-sweet voice of his. "All right. I think, Mr. Bahr, that that's all we need from you today—"

The phone rang, loud and insistent. Libby took the receiver. "For you, Julian. Your office. They say crash priority."

Bahr took the phone. He listened for a moment, and his breathing seemed to stop. "You're certain of that?" he said harshly. "The *moon?* All right, get the report, and every possible observer by direct wire to my office. Contact Englehardt and the Joint Chiefs for conference in sixty minutes. Broadcast a Condition B on all channels. Then contact the Chief Executive and tell him to have a joint session assembled in Washington in…" he glanced at his watch, "…two hours."

He hung up then, and slowly turned to Adams. "All right," he said savagely, almost gleefully. "Get your injunction, if you can. But do it fast, because if you don't have it enforced sixty minutes from now, it will be too late."

He stalked from the room, and the door crashed behind him.

CHAPTER FOURTEEN
Catastrophe

NO CONDITION B blackout could ever have hidden the catastrophe that blazed like a banner in the sky, and Bahr watched impatiently as the Congressmen clumped in little nervous knots here and there, jamming the aisles and doorways of the House chamber.

The session with the Joint Chiefs in New York, with Adams of DEPCO conspicuous by his absence, had been stormy; mostly they objected to calling a joint session of Congress, because Congress had no power to do anything about it anyway, but Bahr had insisted that only a return to the half-forgotten formalities and traditions could really drive home to all the people what had to be done. Congress still nominally represented the people, even though it had no real function anymore.

And the Joint Chiefs finally had given in, because they had to, because they had all seen the Moon in the sky. But not a Moon any longer, just a clump of shattered pieces hanging obediently in orbit like the fragments of a broken plate, slowly falling away from each other...

An observatory in Australia had seen the explosion, a sudden flash of incredible whiteness bursting out in the dark Australian sky, and then, dimly, through the curtain of debris, a mammoth slow motion display of planetary destruction. Idiotic destruction, destruction without point or reason, but destruction with terrible implications.

If the Aliens could do that to the Moon...

From the prop room behind the rostrum Bahr saw the Chief Executive arrive, very splendid and dashing.

Bahr glanced at Libby. "Pretty boy," he said.

"He's cute," Libby said. "No spine, though."

Behind the Chief Executive, the Joint Chiefs, marching down the aisle like the horsemen of the Apocalypse. The roll call was taken; there was a simple introduction from the Speaker of the House. "Julian Bahr, Director DIA, has requested this emergency session to speak to you." Then Bahr was on the rostrum.

Behind him, on a vast screen on the wall, images sprang to life. First a night wirephoto of the fragmented Moon. A slow dissolve into, a chrome-color montage of panic...long ragged evacuation columns, people jammed into the streets, panicky, desperately moving out of the city...rioting crowds at night, brandishing torches...bombed out buildings bursting into flame...shock troops moving in with machine guns and burps...a man in a white shirt running screaming and bloody-faced through a gauntlet of jeering men and women...all hand-picked scenes from the cruel bloody days of the Crash, flashing on the screen, then dimming slowly as Bahr's voice rose in the microphone.

"We have seen these things before, in a time of terror, and we pledged ourselves they would never happen again on the face of the Earth. Now, today, we are threatened again with panic and horror. Whatever the nature of the Alien creatures that have come into our skies, we know what they are attempting to do. We are fighting a war of nerves. Every move the Aliens have made has been calculated to spread panic and terror among us, to force us to destroy ourselves. We have not returned a single blow."

He paused to let that sink in.

"In facing an Alien invader, we have been helpless," he went on. "Where the Aliens are, what they are, how they communicate, what they intend to do...we do not know. This latest blow is a mockery. We are powerless to retaliate. Now we are faced with an inescapable choice. We can wait for the next blow, and the next, and ultimately succumb...or we can carry the attack to the Aliens."

Bahr delivered the line down, so there was no applause, only a long tense silence as the idea sank in. Then: "There is only one way we can do that, only one weapon that can save us." He turned and pointed to the wall screen behind him.

On the screen a gleaming silver image had appeared, the old, almost forgotten spaceship, the XAR5, beginning its takeoff from the New Mexico desert, the ancient film showing in colored slow motion the belching of the engines, the dust cloud. Bahr signaled, and the roar of the massive engines was amplified to deafening volume, cutting all conversation, all thinking to a standstill, the fiery white blast of the jets blinding and fas-cinating. The huge ship rose slowly, the camera panning upwards, the motors screaming, heat waves and sound waves scorching the air, rising, and finally vanishing out of sight.

The screen darkened.

"That," Bahr said, "could have been the most powerful military weapon in history. Had it succeeded, it would have been impregnable, irresistible, omniperceptive. It failed. If the time had been right, space would have been conquered in the nineties, but the time was not right, and we all have bitter memories of that era.

"But that was thirty years ago...thirty years of control, balance, and evolution. Because of the Crash, this entire area of our culture has been held taboo, while we turned our energies inward. We wanted stability, no matter what the cost. All right...now we can see the cost. But now we must fight for survival, and that means we must build that spaceship again if we hope to survive. A spaceship that will work can be assembled and launched in three months. Until that day we are defenseless. But it is within your power to initiate this great military and scientific project again. This is the time to use your power!"

The cheering rose to a deafening roar as they rose from their seats. Bahr was gone from the rostrum long before the noise had subsided, and when the Chief Executive was finally able to secure the attention of the Congress, he read a short, simple request for congressional action. "I propose that the Chief Executive be granted full authority in this emergency to establish a project which shall be called Project Tiger, for the development of a spaceship, and subsequently a space armada, to hunt out and destroy the Alien enemy in his lair, and that this project be placed under the special supervision of the Joint Chiefs and Julian Bahr, Director DIA, to take precedence over every other jurisdiction and activity until this emergency is at an end."

There could be no doubt...

Later, in an anteroom that was crowded with people, Bahr pulled off his coat, drenched with sweat, and loosened his tightly strapped Markheim. Libby was staring at him, wide-eyed. When he came into the room there had been a silence, broken by a rising buzz of excited conversation as the immensity, the swiftness, of the thing began to dawn. Something that could not have happened had happened; it was, incredibly, the end of an era.

Reporters were crowding the room, flashbulbs snapping as statements were distributed. Carl Englehardt was there, shaking Bahr's hand vigorously, pounding him on the back. Two of his DIA men crossed over to him, congratulated him, and said something in low voices. Bahr frowned, his eyes searching across the room.

Near the doorway he saw a thin-faced man waiting.

"Kocek!" Bahr pulled away from the clump of people surrounding him. In the temporary privacy of the hallway, Bahr turned.

"Carmine broke," Kocek said. "Before he died, he talked."

Bahr nodded, a hard smile crossing his face. "Who was it? Who was backing him? Who put him up to it?"

Kocek jerked his head toward the clamoring, racket-filled room. "It was Englehardt," he said. "Carl Englehardt."

CHAPTER FIFTEEN
The Plotters

THERE was darkness, and pain—then the sudden, startling realization that he could move his body again. Tentatively, Harvey Alexander tried. It hurt to breathe; there was a lancinating spasm of pain through his chest. He lay back again panting and trembling.

There was a hospital smell here, but it was not a hospital room. There were bandages on his head and chest, stiffness in his right arm, and a slow dripping bottle of intravenous fluid above his right shoulder.

The fire! There had been a fire, and he had tried to reach the door, and then what? Memories—a kaleidoscopic blaze of fragments without time-relationships. The metallic voice of his interrogators, the questions, and the darkness. Muffled voices above, the endless clack-clack-clack of some kind of machinery, traffic sounds outside.

And later, the harsh ripping sound of stunners on the floor above, the screams, the crackle of flames, the heat.

There were other memories, fuzzy, incoherent. Arms lifting him up from somewhere, carrying him somewhere. The flicker of city lights and colored neons through a car window, silent men on either side of him. More darkness, a room, muffled voices, pain, unconsciousness again. Once, a hurried consultation with words that stuck in his memory: "...alive?" "Yes...deep shock...touch and go..." A woman's presence, and later a man's voice saying, "That will be all, Sister, I'll notify you when I leave..."

His mind caught at it, held it. A pleasant, modulated voice. "Sister" was not American slang, not in that voice, yet the woman was not a nun...the key fell into the lock, a perfect fit, and Alexander opened his eyes, saw the fuzzy male figure near the bed.

"BRINT?" he said.

The man nodded. "Yes, of course. If you feel you can talk now, Major..."

Alexander had never seen the man, who called himself MacKenzie. He learned that he was in the BRINT building of the British Embassy Compound in New York. He had been there for three days, and until eight hours before they had not known if he would live or die.

"We were looking for you almost as soon as our net picked up the story on the Wildwood raid," MacKenzie told him in his soft Scottish burr, "and of course Bahr was looking for you too, which made the problem relatively simple, up to a point. We planned to let him find you, then close in."

MacKenzie grinned ruefully. "We didn't realize then that you were to be used as bait in conspiracy from within the DIA to unseat Bahr. We didn't realize that anybody, even Bahr, thought you were that important. And we didn't know that Bahr would make such a fast personal move to smash the insurrection. Fortunately, we had the wit to get you out of there before you were completely incinerated."

"Yes." Alexander flexed his still-stiff arm. "What I can't quite see is why. Why all your interest in me at all?"

"Because we couldn't risk letting you contact your own Army CI or DEPCO until we knew for certain just why Julian Bahr was so fantastically interested in having you caught."

"Not caught," Alexander said flatly. "Killed. Or at least, recooped."

"But why? Because of something you knew about the Wildwood raid?" MacKenzie asked.

"Bahr wanted my *mind* out of commission. He was afraid of what I might be able to figure out—eventually—on the basis of what I knew."

"Ah," MacKenzie said softly. "Now we are approaching it. What might you have been able to figure out?"

"The truth about what happened at Wildwood. The Wildwood incident was the key to the whole thing."

MacKenzie poured Scotch in a couple of glasses, handed one to Alexander. "Do you mind if I record this?"

"If you expect proof, I don't have it. But certain things I *know* are true. For instance I know that no U-metal was stolen from Wildwood. I designed the security system there, and I knew a few things about it that Bahr and his DIA men didn't know. By the same token, the Alien raiders would not have known those things either. Now, what actually happened at Wildwood? An alarm went off outside the compound, there was an explosion several miles away, and subsequently a shortage of U-metal was discovered inside the plant. The inference was that the radioactives detected outside the compound were the same as those missing inside, and that the theft was accomplished by humanoid Aliens, or a human agent, who smuggled the material through the Geiger monitors by means of some kind of shielding."

The BRINT man nodded. "A collapsed neutronic shield is the popular rumor, I believe. A shield a few nuclei thick that would have all the stopping power of a huge block of concrete."

"And even if it were tissue-paper thin, it would still weigh as much as a four-foot slab of lead," Harvey Alexander said.

MacKenzie blinked; then he was roaring with laughter. "Of course it's obvious," he said. "Once it's pointed out. They'll have a fit back home, for not noticing that."

"The rest wasn't so obvious," Alexander continued, "but it made sense when you thought it through. Without a shield, no U-metal came through those gates. Therefore, the hot stuff that set off the road monitor was not the U-metal that was later found missing in the Plant. So the three missing slugs must have been disposed of inside the Plant, probably dumped down the refuse pipes leading to the waste dump. But if that was what happened, then the raid on the Wildwood Plant had to be a forgery. And if that raid was something that was deliberately staged, then Project Frisco must have been staged from beginning to end. And that was what Bahr was afraid I would figure out. That the Alien invasion has been a hoax from the beginning. There aren't any Aliens."

Alexander turned to MacKenzie then, and set his drink carefully down on the table. "I also think that BRINT knows that is true, and has known it from the start. But I could be wrong, of course."

"Oh, no," MacKenzie said slowly. "You aren't wrong. And you can see why we could not afford to have you place your deductions in the hands of DEPCO." The BRINT man's voice was suddenly tired, and tinged with bitterness. "We've been playing a long gamble, and it seemed as though we were winning, at least at first. But now we've come to the really big question, and we don't have the one answer that we really have to have." He looked at Alexander. "How to stop Julian Bahr."

"We needed a wedge," MacKenzie said later, "to smash

through the wall that DEPCO had built around itself. A balance of power can be maintained only if the two sides of the balance are very nearly equal. On one side we saw the Eastern Bloc, pulling out of the Crash with a burgeoning military machine and an aggressive totalitarian government. We were able to hold the Eastern Bloc in check—*barely* hold it in check— by the threat of the Robling missiles. But on the other side, in Federation America, we saw DEPCO grow and expand, entrenching itself more and more firmly as the all-powerful, controlling Bureau in the government, following its course of stability at any cost and gradually dragging the whole Western economy to a standstill."

The Scotsman poured another drink. "We could see it happening on all sides. Nobody dared guess where it might have ended if it had gone on undisturbed, but anyone whose head was not buried in the system could see how it entrenched itself more firmly every year.

"Every frontier, every challenge was systematically being sliced away, every sign of progress curbed. This was not Vanner's plan. He saw the stability period as a transition.

"It didn't work that way. How soon the society would have disintegrated completely, nobody knows. But it was clear that a frontier had to be established again, before it was too late."

"A space frontier?"

"Anything would have done it," MacKenzie said, "as long as it was a frontier. Some drive that would require a massive national effort to achieve. A war would have meant the certain destruction of Federation America. Only one challenge was big enough. But a drive to space was the one thing, above all things, that DEPCO would block at any cost. The fear and suspicion of spaceships that was engendered by the Crash was not a rational fear, but that didn't matter. It was real."

"So Bahr was your wedge," Alexander said.

"Bahr was our wedge. Carl Englehardt didn't recognize the peril in the same terms we did, but he wanted the spaceship project reestablished. His motives were completely personal and

Libby screamed her hatred as she slashed Adams' face.

individual; the important thing was that he thought he knew a way to force a reopening of the project. He knew a young, ambitious man in the DIA, a man who was strong enough, and tough enough, and ruthless enough to drive a hole through DEPCO's wall of over-regulation and smash it down. Englehardt gave him a toehold, a series of carefully staged incidents which led, by inference, to the conclusion that we were on the eve of an Alien invasion."

"Then Englehardt prepared the 'ships' that exploded?" Alexander asked. "What about the Moon?"

"Remember that Englehardt has been making intercontinental missiles for years, capable of carrying fusion warheads. It was no problem to place half a dozen unmanned drones on the Moon. The difficult part—in which BRINT cooperated—was handling the leaking of information that followed each successive incident. Bahr knew it was a hoax, and it fit into his plans perfectly. Once started, it all followed nicely...the circulation of a pulp scare-book, to prepare the public for the panic that would follow; the step-by-step creation of a national peril that could be met and answered only by a drive to build a space fleet.

"Vanner had proved that the conquest of space would ultimately require a national effort comparable to a full scale war, but if Federation America were to support it, it had to be an emotional cause, a fear-cause with a leader who could draw the people along and supply the great force needed to burst through thirty years of entrenched anti-space conditioning."

MacKenzie spread his hands. "We needed a man with the drive and strength to leap into the breach and use the crisis. We had to have Bahr. But he moved too fast, he was too successful. He didn't fight DEPCO the way we expected him to. He simply walked around DEPCO and left them standing there. Earlier, we might have been able to control him. Now he is out of control, and in a matter of weeks he will have a continent under his thumb, and a military and technical program straining the nation to its limits. In six months he will want the world, and we won't be able to stop him…

"Can't Englehardt stop him?" Alexander asked.

MacKenzie gave him an odd look.

"Englehardt is dead," he said slowly. "He was shot down on the street by unidentified assassins an hour after Bahr made his appeal to Congress." The BRINT man shrugged. "Bahr immediately nationalized Robling holdings by edict, and doubled the pay of every man in the organization."

The two men sat silent for a few moments. "It seems to me," Alexander said, "that the job is only half done. You have to leave Bahr in power until he's carried Project Tiger to a fruitful point."

"And shaken the government apart, and entrenched himself like an iron fist? What do we do when Project Tiger is half completed, and Bahr has made himself invincible?"

"Then we dump him," Alexander said.

MacKenzie looked at the Major's face, and realized that he was serious. "How?"

"I have an idea," Alexander said. "I think Julian Bahr's great strength can be his weakness. I'll need help, but if I'm right, when the time comes, I'll dump Julian Bahr."

"At the height of his power?" MacKenzie asked.

"The tragic hero," said Alexander.

CHAPTER SIXTEEN
Escape

LIBBY ALLISON watched Julian Bahr in horror and fascination. There had been times when she had seen this clearly, the thing that had been coming from the very first. Now, suddenly, all the restraints were broken, all the barriers down. He had stamped and pounded and bulldozed through the field, and suddenly it was empty before him, he was in command. He stood there, talking, his ego swelling, power and confidence in every word, every movement of his head, every gesture of his hands…and still he was driving forward, fighting.

He will change the whole country into a dynasty, she thought. He will set civilization back six hundred years. There will be no stopping him. He is thirty-four years old, and in a week he will be ruling a continent, but that will not be enough. He could be the master of the world, and that would not be enough. By the time he is fifty, the idolatry of ten billion people might still make him feel unloved.

When Julian was at her side, taking her arm through the crowds, she realized with shock that she was proud of him, excited for him, eager for him. He had fought so hard and he had won, in spite of everything. Now he was making her a part of the victory.

His white goddess. His empress. His wife, his lover, his concubine, his first love, his partner, his daughter, his sister, his mother—

The dream exploded with sudden brutality and the vast panoramic nightmare-lens clamped down to a tight, narrow channel and came into focus on Adams' face.

Adams, pushing his way through the room, his coat lapels flapping, his face white, distorted, ugly. He thrust at the crowds of people that were intervening, and they stepped back as his anger swept the room like a wave. He approached Julian Bahr, and two of Bahr's men appeared at Adams' side, suddenly, each taking an arm, holding him as he writhed to break away. But his hate-filled eyes were not turned toward Bahr at all, they were turned toward Libby.

"You bitch!" he screamed, lunging forward to glare into her face. "You bitch! You did it! Aren't you proud! Vanner should be proud of his bastard daughter. Oh, yes, he should be proud, and your slut mother, too! You've betrayed everything they ever believed in, and now see what you've won for yourself."

She had a drink in her hand, and she hit him in the face with it so hard that the glass shattered. Something snapped in her mind, and she threw herself on Adams, gashing his face again and again with the broken glass, pouring out all the hatred she had ever felt.

Then she heard somebody screaming, and it was Adams, and his face looked like the skin had been hacked off. She stepped back, gasping, and at her side Bahr was laughing, and the DIA men were grinning at her and holding Adams so he couldn't move, and Adams kept screaming, "Traitor! Traitor!"

Then Bahr nodded, a curt order, and the men dragged Adams out through the doorway and Libby was sick—more violently sick than she had ever been in her life—and somebody was helping her across the room, into a lavatory. In the mirror she saw herself, and there was blood all over her hands and arms and dress, and some of it was her blood, but most of it was Adams'.

All the way home, through the dark wet streets, something in her mind was screaming at her that the nightmare was real, the nightmare was real, the nightmare was real...

Bahr didn't notice that she was gone for quite a long time, and then only vaguely, as he caught himself looking around the room, trying to find her. He chuckled to himself. She had turned on Adams, all right. He hadn't thought that she had it in her, and he felt his pride swell as he thought of it. He'd been right about Libby. She would help him. She knew the DEPCO organization, she would know whom to keep, whom to get rid of. With Libby at his side—

But she was not in the room, and he spoke to one of his men, who vanished for five minutes or so, then returned, frowning.

"She's gone, Chief. She left the lavatory, and somebody saw her hail a cab outside..."

"Get a car," he said, "and get these parasites out of here."

How long had it been since she left? He tried to wade through the drunken exhilaration of the past hours, and he couldn't remember. He snarled at the driver and slammed his fist into his palm.

Outside the apartment building he leaped from the car, jammed the elevator button with his thumb, then cursed and started up the stairs three at a time, with his men panting behind him. He ran down the corridor. He stopped at the apartment door. It was open.

Inside there was nothing. She was gone. The closet doors hung open, clothes gone as though grabbed up in a desperate sweep of the hand. A suitcase was gone from the shelf. Dresser drawers yawned at him, empty, and in the back room the crib was also empty—

He stared at the room, unable to believe what he saw. He was trembling; he couldn't control the shaking of his hands, and he saw his face in the mirror and slammed off the light switch with a snarl of rage.

She was gone as if she had never been there.

He drove his fist down on the table, snapping a leg and splintering the top.

Libby had walked out on him! After all he had done for her, even after what had happened tonight, she had walked out, left him flat, turned her back on him!

But she would pay for it. She would suffer, and then when he was through with her, there was the boy.

He turned to his men, and swiftly, carefully, he began giving his orders.

CHAPTER SEVENTEEN
Rogue Tiger

EVEN Alexander and MacKenzie had not anticipated the speed with which Bahr would move. For MacKenzie, there was endless work in the BRINT field offices; for Alexander, a growing desperate urgency, to crystallize the plan he had seen only in its barest outlines.

He spent days studying the fat dossier on Julian Bahr from the BRINT top-sec files, and through it all he saw the governmental structure of Federation America tremble, totter and crumble under the driving force of Project Tiger.

The changes were sweeping, and fundamental. With the

Robling combine under Bahr's personal control, the first moves were swift. At White Sands, for thirty years a ghost town, the gutted and abhorred remains of the old XAR project were exhumed. White Sands became a metropolis.

As the Project got going, the research chief for the defense section of the old DEPEX rose in protest. "What you're proposing is impossible," he told Bahr in the hot, crowded conference room one morning. "The economy can't support it. It would require an effort equivalent to a major war."

"We are engaged in a major war," Bahr said, "and there will have to be changes in the economy."

"But the changes you are talking about will reduce the population to starvation level..."

"We have no choice," Bahr said. "Above all, we cannot afford to sentimentalize." The DEPEX man was retired from his post, and Bahr named a replacement.

Bahr's manner of dealing with DEPCO was simple. He cut off their funds. The economy, he told them, was being reorganized to accomplish Project Tiger, and long-range research programs—which would not contribute to the major effort—were being indefinitely suspended.

And through it all, an infiltration of trusted DIA men began into the bureaus, the planning commissions, the offices, and a slow, inexorable tightening of control began, a rerouting of the channels of authority upward into the hands of a single man. There were more Alien incidents, with the usual publicity and no captures, but the panic and terror that ensued was channeled and harnessed in the rigid program that was to rid the skies of the Aliens forever.

It was a pattern as old as time, moving step by step in its dreadful familiarity, and Alexander and MacKenzie watched it. Every real tyrant in history had followed the pattern. Napoleon, Hitler, Stalin, Mikoyan—they all knew it well.

But to Julian Bahr a far more important war, a private, personal war, was progressing, and he drove his fist into his hand again and again as his rage burned brighter and brighter.

It took Harvey Alexander almost a week to pick up Libby's trail, but he finally located her in a rundown Boston suburban apartment house.

When he was finally certain that she was not under DIA stakeout, he went up to the third-floor room, and knocked.

She was staggering drunk, and her voice was hoarse and ragged. "You want something?" she said harshly. "I don't want to stand in this doorway all night."

Alexander pushed past her into the filthy room and closed the door. She went across to the half-finished drink on the bureau. "Who asked you in here?" Then she turned, frightened. "DIA?"

"Make some coffee," Alexander said. "I want to talk."

"Thanks, I'll stay drunk."

He hit her viciously across the face, and dragged her by the collar of her bathrobe over to the wash basin. He made her throw up, and wiped her face off with a wet towel. He made some surro-coffee, and she sat bent over drinking it, her eyes closed, tired and defeated and sick. She threw up the second cup before she was sober; her face was dead with exhaustion and fear. "Who are you? What do you want? Why can't you leave me alone?"

Alexander shook his head. Her red hair, was an unkempt mop, and her mouth sagged open in a stupid, beaten expression. He saw the bruise under one eye, the black and blue marks on her neck. "Clean up and get some clothes on," he said. "You make me sick to look at you."

It was bad, far worse than he had expected. How could a woman go to pieces like that? He paced the floor, lit a cigarette, wondering if he had made a terrible error. He needed her, everything he had planned depended on her, but she would have to be strong, not broken and washed out—

Clothes and makeup helped some. She seemed a little more alive when she reappeared.

He stood up. "All right, my name is Alexander, and I'm not DIA," he told her. "I'm with Army Intelligence, assigned to

BRINT. I want to talk to you, but it's nearly dinnertime. I have a car outside. Where do you want to eat?"

Libby looked at him for a moment, confused and disbelieving, her face colored. Then she seemed to stand a little straighter, to look more like the attractive, intelligent girl the BRINT dossier had described.

"I know a place—"

He didn't question her that night, even though he was eager to sound her out. She was exhausted. But the morning saw a new person. The apartment was in order, and she offered him coffee.

They talked, and Alexander told her enough to make it clear that he knew a great deal about her, and about Bahr.

And then, quite abruptly, the pain and terrible grief came out in a torrent, a storm of emotion that she had been trying to hold in. Alexander listened, and knew for the first time that he was going to win.

"I knew he would be angry when I left him," she said. "I didn't realize that he would be so violently, vindictively furious. The morning after I left, he cancelled DEPCO. He cancelled my clearance and my stability rating. That first day his men found out where I was staying; when I came back home my car had been stolen and my apartment looted. I took Timmy and found another place. I thought if we could just wait it out for a few days, it would blow over..."

She looked up at Alexander, the fear and grief still in her eyes. "I was wrong, oh, but I was wrong! The second day they attached my bank account, and I had no money. That afternoon the police came, with a committee of Education and Conditioning people. I didn't have a job; I didn't have an income, so obviously I could not adequately support a child. They took Tim away. I thought I knew Julian, but I couldn't believe that he'd let his own son go into the Playschool system. He did it just to hurt me. Inside of three days I didn't have enough money to eat with. Then Bahr nationalized my apartment building, and I was out. He put in this miserable currency reform, and I didn't have a bond or security that was worth the paper it was written on. Even my life insurance—"

She broke off, and poured herself a drink.

"Why did you leave him?" Alexander asked.

"I wish I knew that. I wish I knew, for sure." The girl threw herself down on the sofa. "Mark Vanner—he wasn't really my uncle, but he brought me up from the time I was a little girl. He was a national figure when Julian Bahr was a scrawny little road-rat. Mark Vanner held this country together for years on just faith, and respect, and decent honest leadership. Do you think Julian Bahr could have done that?" She spread her hands helplessly. "Vanner was a man, a magnificent man. When he became Chief of Economic Planning there wasn't a factory in operation anywhere in the country. He didn't have money, or a gang of gunmen to back him up. But he talked to people, and he went around to the colleges and defense agencies, and the people volunteered by the hundreds and thousands. Sincere people who believed in Mark Vanner and believed that his social-economic system was the only thing that could pull us together again. Harrison, Kronsky, Williams, Otto Lieblitz…my mother and father before they were killed…those were the kind of people who started DEPCO."

It was silent in the room, and outside the rain was coming down against the window. "They worked for five years," Libby went on. "They built this country up again, from a dying giant to a prosperous, stable world power. It was only supposed to be a temporary measure, a chance for the country to get back on its feet again. And then Julian Bahr came into power. He hated DEPCO, and he was afraid of DEPCO, and in one week he destroyed the organization that it took us twenty-five years to build."

"But the DEPCO organization wasn't all good," Alexander said.

"Of course it wasn't all good but the point is, it wasn't all bad, either. And me, I was the fool, the wide-eyed virgin." She bit her lip. "I was terribly in love with him when we first met, and I told myself lies about him and made myself believe things that never could have been true. But then, when he had broken down DEPCO, even I couldn't pretend to myself any longer. When I found myself standing there deliberately mutilating a man that I hated, I knew if I stayed with Bahr I would have to destroy things the way *he* wants to destroy things. I had already compromised DEPCO and broken every promise and moral contract I'd ever made, and betrayed everything I'd ever believed in."

She took a deep breath, and spread her hands again. "I knew then that I couldn't do it, and it wouldn't make any difference what he did to me, no matter how much he hated me, I couldn't do it."

She gave a brittle laugh. "There isn't much more. I got out of New York. The police had me in for questioning twice. I saw he wasn't going to quit, not until I was pounded right down into the ground. I stole a car and drove to Boston and ran the car into the river. I had no money and no papers, so I couldn't get a job. I didn't dare register for relief, because Bahr would find me. There isn't any work for me here. I have three college degrees and an IQ of 150, and I can't even get a job as a waitress. I hadn't eaten for two days when I got to Boston, but I found a way to live. No papers, no clearance, I can't even be a registered slut, so I take what I can get. I'm young, I learn fast, I'm scared sick and I get myself drunk as much as I can stand it, I hate myself, but I swear I hate him worse."

Alexander waited until he was certain that the time was right. Then he said, "I think that I might be able to find out where your son is."

"He's somewhere in the Playschool system," she said, hardly daring to believe what she heard. "The records will have been changed."

"I know that. I still think we could locate him. If he is in the system, BRINT will have duplicate files."

If they could locate the boy, BRINT would get him out of

the Playschool. Money would be made available, and Libby and Tim would be conducted out of the country, probably to Canada. In return, Libby would help Alexander.

"How?" she wanted to know.

"It has to do with Bahr. I can't tell you more right now, except that it may be dangerous for you."

"And Tim will be gotten out of the School in any case?"

"Before anything else begins," Alexander promised her. "But you may have to face Bahr personally. And fight him. If you're afraid to, you'd better say so now."

Libby was silent for a long time. Then she turned away. "I don't want anything to do with Bahr," she said dully.

"All right. But what are you going to do with your life, then? Drink yourself blind? Forget Bahr and your son? Look...you're part of this. Julian Bahr didn't just happen out of a clear blue sky. You made him. DEPCO made him. Vanner—yes, Mark Vanner made him, hate by hate."

"I know that," she said sharply. "I know what DEPCO did to him when he was in Riley...he was washed up when I met him. I made him stand up again. I made him fight—" She stopped.

"Yes, you made him fight, to build an empire to lay at your feet." Alexander faced her, forced her to meet his eyes. "Do you know why you ran away from Bahr? I'll tell you why. Because you'd already destroyed DEPCO. You always wanted to."

"I didn't! I wanted to help, to do all I could—"

"By shielding Bahr? By putting him in power?"

She whirled on him. "Why do you want to torment me? I hate you!"

"You hate Bahr. Fight him."

"All right, I will. I'll get even with him—" she bit off the rest of the sentence, but her eyes were narrowing and hardening in anger, and Alexander knew that the White Queen was already taken.

It had gone smoothly for Bahr during the weeks while the continent was torn, hammered and smelted into a space industry under his ruthless reform. There had been enough work to tax even Bahr's enormous reserves, and exhaustion gave him occasional stretches of dreamless sleep. On his desk was the report from White Sands announcing the first successful pilot model of the new atomic drive, and he was pleased, vastly pleased, until another more private report came into his hands.

He read it, and bellowed for Walters, from whom the report had come. "What does this thing mean?"

"Just what it says," Walters told him. "She took the child back."

"What do you mean, she took the child back? Who said she could take the child back?"

Walters showed him the papers.

It was perfectly legal and straightforward. An attorney representing Libby Allison had paid a quiet visit to the authorities at the Bordentown Playschool. He had made the proper identification in Libby's behalf, and presented satisfactory evidence of her desire and ability to support the child properly. She had a sufficiently good job and a suitable standing account in a Canadian bank. The paperwork had been carried through, and Tim had been released in her care.

Bahr alerted four of his men and ordered them to make an investigative pounce.

They found her apartment in Boston, but Libby Allison was gone. Her forwarding address was in Quebec, Canada. A check with the Border Guard Intelligence gave the tantalizing information that Libby had driven into Canada with a permanent residence passport the previous day.

The boy had been with her.

The very audacity of it infuriated Bahr even more than the fact itself. A conference was made with Braelow, his personal attorney, where he laid it on the line. "I want that boy back here. I don't care how, I don't even care whether he's dead or alive, *I just want him back!*"

Braelow studied the situation, and came back with empty hands. Libby had a job; she left Tim in a nursery during the day, and took him home to an apartment a few blocks away at night. Her Canadian job was actually civil service; Bahr put pressure on various people to get her fired, but something or somebody seemed to be exerting equal pressure on the other side.

He tried diplomatic channels, demanding to have Libby extradited on legal and political charges, but this curiously came to a dead end, and the Legation, in a huff, returned him a sharp warning against trying to violate political sanctuary.

Then he received a personal letter from Libby, through her attorneys. Bahr read it, and tore it into shreds. Shortly thereafter he planned the kidnapping.

His DIA men did not return at the appointed time; in fact, they did not return at all, so he did not know exactly what had gone wrong. But not only did the kidnapping mission fail, the incident hit the newspapers, and the Canadian police found out somehow that there was a DIA linkage in the kidnapping attempt. Although it was only rumor and completely unconfirmed by Canadian officials, the European news nets played the story up as fact; quite suddenly Bahr found the devoted public of Federation America catching the scent of scandal and looking to him confidently for explanation.

He faced Braelow in private conference. "I want that boy back," he said furiously.

Braelow spread his hands. "There isn't any way but a court fight," he said. "She's deliberately turning this into a dirty mess. It's impossible…"

It was the wrong thing to say. "I said I wanted the boy back," Bahr grated. "Set up any kind of case you have to, but get him back."

"You mean you'd let it go into court?"

"Good lord, are you deaf? No common, low-grade tramp is going to—" Bahr broke off, incoherent. "You heard what I said. Now do it."

Braelow and his staff mounted the case.

Julian Bahr of course, tried every conceivable device to keep the affair out of the courts.

But Libby would not meet with him or his attorneys directly; her counsel was from the best legal firm in Canada. With no other alternative at his disposal, Bahr bent every effort toward a quick, quiet settlement before a Canadian judge, confident that BURINF could do a neat job of cover up for him on the American side.

Consequently, he received a bad jolt when he walked into the courtroom with Braelow at his elbow, and found himself facing a battery of 3-V cameras and microphones, with the press-box packed with journalists from five continents waiting patiently for the fun to begin…

He caught Braelow's arm. "What are those cameras doing in here?" he whispered furiously. "Those newsmen…this is my fight, my personal, private fight…"

"You have nothing personal or private anymore," Braelow told him coldly. "You might as well get that through your head. We're on thin ice out here, and it's out of our control. The cameras were the judge's option, and he insisted on having them here so there wouldn't be any kickback later."

"All right, then, get my men to work jamming any broadcast," Bahr said.

"They've tried it already, and they can't. Radio Budapest is getting through, and so are half a dozen other foreign nets." Braelow shrugged. "According to Intelligence, most of the population is following the news, one way or another."

Bahr cursed. "How is this thing going to go?"

"Maybe not too bad," Braelow said. "And we have a terrific edge on the support aspect. The woman's job here will hardly clothe and feed the child, much less educate him. That's plainly one of our best cards."

"You play the cards, don't bother me with them," Bahr said tightly. "Just so we win…"

In another room in the courthouse, Libby turned to Harvey Alexander. "I'm afraid," she said. "I don't know if I can face him."

He put his hand on her shoulder. Her whole body was shaking. "Look," he said, kindly, "I'll be doing the court fighting, and either you have confidence in me, or you don't..."

"It isn't that," Libby said miserably. "It's the whole idea. The thing we're going to do to him. It's brutal."

"I know it."

"And it's a *lie.*"

Alexander shrugged. "I wouldn't do it if I knew any other way to make him break. But it doesn't matter now whether we like it or not. I've shown you the BRINT reports."

"I know, I know," Libby said. "We have to get Julian out now." She looked helplessly at Alexander. "I hate him, believe me, I hate him, but what will happen to him? And what if it doesn't work?"

"If it doesn't work, we've got nothing to lose anyway. He'll expand into Canada, and then Europe, and nothing you or I can do then will make the slightest difference. We have to get him now, before he's entrenched. Look, Libby, it's up to you. You've got to do it, or we're through."

"There must be some other way..."

"We got Tim out of the Playschool and into Canada." Alexander said, trying to sound confident. "BRINT folded up the kidnapping attempt without a hitch. So far we've blocked Bahr at every turn. You must have known what you were doing when you started...are you going to quit now, and let him take you like he's always taken you?"

Libby flushed. "No," she said.

There was a hushed murmur as she appeared in the courtroom. Cameras of two continents swung toward her as she walked toward the table near the front of the room. She saw Bahr's eyes meet hers, contemptuously, and then widen; his face turned a sudden angry red and he almost leaped to his feet when he saw that her counsel was a lean, bronzed Harvey Alexander, in the uniform of a general in U. S. Army Intelligence, complete with combat braid and decorations...

Alexander took the opening advantage by putting Bahr on the defensive. "What was your reaction to the attempted kidnapping of Miss Allison's child?"

"I was naturally concerned," Bahr said, "and I would like to add that I am exceedingly grateful to the Canadian authorities, who were alert enough to prevent what might have been a tragic incident."

"Can you think of any reason why someone should have wanted to carry out this kidnapping, Mr. Bahr?"

"I cannot, unless they knew he was my son and intended to bilk me for ransom."

"Then someone must have been aware of your earlier attempt to negotiate with Miss Allison?"

Bahr reddened. "That's possible. It was a domestic matter, I made no attempt at secrecy."

Alexander's voice was smooth. "Could some overzealous people have attempted the kidnapping, thinking they were acting in your interests?"

"I think not," Bahr said sharply. "My people know I don't operate that way and they are completely loyal."

Alexander let that remark sink home; then he thrust the knife. "In that case, I'm sure you can explain," he said, "why every member of the kidnapping group was an agent in the New York division of your own DIA...!"

During the recess Bahr had a background check run on Alexander, on a crash priority, intent on discrediting him as an imposter. Alexander was a passed-over Major in the Army, a deserter, and wanted by the DIA for stability check and Alien contact. A General! Bahr snorted.

The background check altered his plans. The Army records were complete and perfect. Alexander, they said, had been on special CI assignment since the Wildwood raid; his promotion had been reconsidered, and he had been spot-promoted to General.

The escape from Kelley was no help, since Alexander had been registered there under a John Smith label for Bahr's convenience. As far as the records were concerned, the incident had never happened, and Alexander was legally scot-free. The recess was short, but by the time he went back into court Bahr was certain that some forgery and conniving had been carried out with the Army files. He smelled a rat, but he didn't know what to do about it.

After the recess, the unpleasantness of the opening session intensified. Bahr presented his claims for the boy. Alexander parried every inference against Libby's character and qualifications, but felt that he was losing ground nonetheless. Bahr's confidence was returning; he nodded to his counsel, and they began a long string of male witnesses testifying to Libby's immoral conduct during the past weeks. Alexander appeared confused as the picture developed inexorably. Finally he put Libby herself on the stand.

She tensed herself for the ordeal, to do what she had to do. "I could deny what these men have been saying, but I won't," she said. "When DEPCO was closed down my apartment was looted, my bank account frozen, and I was turned out on the street. My education kept me out of low-skilled jobs, and my red security card, a present from Mr. Bahr, kept me out of highly skilled jobs, and when the currency was changed, well, show me one person in Federation America who didn't go through hell during that changeover..."

She saw Bahr's face go red with anger, saw the cameras watching her from four angles across the room. Her low voice now raised so it carried across the courtroom. "But we're not talking about me, we're talking about this man's claim on my son. I've been insulted, attacked, and my private life put under the spotlight all on the strength of the sanctimonious claims of this man. Well, I would like to ask Mr. Bahr if he has one shred of proof—even a single scrap of paper that will prove that he is the father of my child."

There was a stunned silence. Then Bahr was on his feet. "This is ridiculous," he roared. "There are the paternity papers!" He broke off suddenly, staring at the cameras, his mouth still open.

He remembered.

There were no paternity papers.

The following day, a barrage of Evidence...blood typing, flesh and hair tests, fingerprint whorls, eye color. Alexander dismissed it all, pleasantly but firmly. "Hundreds of men could have produced a child with these characteristics," he said. "This isn't conclusive. It isn't even evidence at all."

More testimony, not in especially good taste, but Bahr was desperate. He verified the skiing vacation they took when Libby had become pregnant. Witnesses testified that they shared the same room.

Libby shook her head. "What difference does that make?" she asked Braelow. "All you're proving is immorality, not paternity."

"You admit you went on weekends with Mr. Bahr?"

"Certainly."

"That he was intimate with you?"

"So were other men," Libby said, "according to you. You ran a regiment through this courtroom to prove it. Who was in bed with me doesn't matter. What matters is who got me pregnant. It was not Bahr."

Braelow turned back to the table, confused. "All right," Bahr said angrily, "you've messed around long enough." He stood up and strode to the center of the room, glaring at Libby, raising his head to the cameras. He knew the eyes that were watching him, now, but he didn't care any longer, all he could see was her face, her eyes watching him with hatred; all he could feel now was the violent, overpowering urgency to break her, to beat her down and pound her into the ground. He didn't care if the entire world was watching, she couldn't do what she was doing to him and get away with it. "Now," he said, his voice thick with re-pressed anger. "Let's straighten out a few simple facts. Let's talk about the year 2022. That is when you became pregnant, right?"

"In March, to be exact," Libby said.

"Did you arrange to meet me at the ski resort in Sun Valley…and did you not fly out there?"

"Yes."

"We were together for two week ends?"

"Yes."

"And it was during this time that you became pregnant?"

"Well, a woman has to calculate backwards…but I'm certain I became pregnant during that ten days in Sun Valley."

"Then it couldn't have been anybody but me," Bahr said, and stepped back triumphantly.

Libby's answer was mocking laughter. "So I led you to believe."

"You slut!" Bahr screamed, and smashed his hand across her face. She fell out of the chair, and Bahr reached down, grabbed her by the shoulder, drawing his fist back savagely. Someone seized his wrist, twisted it and threw him off balance, and he was glaring into Alexander's face. Suddenly Bahr remembered the cameras. The 3-V lens caught a close-up of his face, hideous with the anger of death.

Then Libby was speaking directly into the 3-V lenses. "He could *never* have been the father of my child." She looked around the room, drawing full attention, and then looked at Bahr, and made a slow, deliberate gesture. There was a gasp from the courtroom.

"He is a fraud," she said, "a magnificent fake. Julian Bahr is impotent."

EPILOGUE.

IT HAD been predictable, and yet unpredictable; he had headed for the border, and then, abruptly, the BRINT patrol had lost him, and it was almost an hour before they realized that he had doubled back, that he had never intended to go to the border at all.

Emergency Director Harvey Alexander arrived in his Volta just as the BRINT men were breaking down the door to Libby's apartment. "The guard," he groaned, "Hell...didn't she even have a guard?"

"She did have," said MacKenzie. "The guard was killed by a silent stunner. A couple of DIA men who were still loyal to him blocked our way up here for fifteen minutes." The BRINT man put a hand on Alexander's shoulder. "I'm sorry," he said. "We thought Bahr would try to get across the border when he slipped away from our patrol."

In the dark hallway the axe-blows on the door shredded the silence. The door crashed in. Two BRINT men pushed through inside, stunners ready. Alexander followed them in.

They were too late.

She lay on the floor. Her face had been beaten to jelly, the flesh and bones mashed beyond recognition as if some blunt heavy maul had been used. She was naked, until they put a sheet over her. Even in death her body was twisted in agony.

Julian Bahr sat in darkness in the next room. The BRINT men surrounded him with drawn guns, but it was a needless gesture. He sat dull and silent, staring at the floor, and his hands were broken and swollen and bloody.

Later, as they were strapping Bahr onto a stretcher, Alexander half listened to the aide speaking into his ear. "...rounded up most of the top DIA men, except those who got to the Southern Continent...no question about your confirmation in the appointment. The engineering people at White Sands have pledged loyalty."

He nodded, but he wasn't hearing. He knew that presently he would have to think about it. There was so much work to be done. The frontier had been reopened; gradually, the pace would be slowed, the starvation economy improved, Project Tiger converted from a crash war operation to a long range program of progress that would ultimately take men out to the stars. He would not have to do it alone; he would have able hands helping him. There was MacKenzie and a dozen, perhaps a hundred men like him.

But now he could think only of Julian Bahr. Bahr was there,

but Bahr did not see him. He did not see Alexander weeping silently and alone over Libby's body, nor turning back to the world and the overwhelming task he had taken on, to hold the reins of power in firm and dedicated hands.

Julian Bahr would not see the great spaceships rise, months and years later, nor would he see his son grow tall and strong. He did not die, but still he was not alive; something had broken within him, the world changed, the days went by, but he did not see, nor understand, for the eyes of Julian Bahr were the eyes of a madman.

But someday, Alexander hoped, Bahr's son would see...and understand.

THE END

If you've enjoyed this book, you will not want to miss these terrific titles...